Jaws of deat

Gadgets heard what sounded like a labored grunt, and what may have been the quick breath of a dog. There was also what may have been a scrape of claws on the concrete, and finally the frenzied snarl of a ravenous beast.

Schwarz couldn't suppress a howl of pain as something bit into his calf. He twisted, frantically kicking at the thing. It was something hard and bony and definitely not human.

He felt a searing pain as needle-sharp teeth sank into his knee, possibly all the way down to the bone. He heard another enraged snarl, and thought, *This thing isn't killing, it's feeding. The goddamn thing is feeding!*

"Able Team will go anywhere, do anything, in order to complete their mission."

—*West Coast Review of Books*

Mack Bolan's

ABLE TEAM®

#1 Tower of Terror
#2 The Hostaged Island
#3 Texas Showdown
#4 Amazon Slaughter
#5 Cairo Countdown
#6 Warlord of Azatlan
#7 Justice by Fire
#8 Army of Devils
#9 Kill School
#10 Royal Flush
#11 Five Rings of Fire
#12 Deathbites
#13 Scorched Earth
#14 Into the Maze
#15 They Came to Kill
#16 Rain of Doom
#17 Fire and Maneuver
#18 Tech War
#19 Ironman
#20 Shot to Hell
#21 Death Strike
#22 The World War III Game
#23 Fall Back and Kill
#24 Blood Gambit
#25 Hard Kill
#26 The Iron God
#27 Cajun Angel
#28 Miami Crush
#29 Death Ride
#30 Hit and Run
#31 Ghost Train
#32 Firecross
#33 Cowboy's Revenge
#34 Clear Shot
#35 Strike Force
#36 Final Run
#37 Red Menace
#38 Cold Steel
#39 Death Code
#40 Blood Mark
#41 White Fire
#42 Dead Zone
#43 Kill Orbit
#44 Night Heat
#45 Lethal Trade
#46 Counterblow
#47 Shadow Warriors
#48 Cult War
#49 Dueling Missiles
#50 Death Hunt
#51 Skinwalker

ABLE TEAM®

Skinwalker

Dick Stivers

TORONTO • NEW YORK • LONDON • PARIS
AMSTERDAM • STOCKHOLM • HAMBURG
ATHENS • MILAN • TOKYO • SYDNEY

First edition January 1991

ISBN 0-373-61251-6

Special thanks and acknowledgment to
Ken Rose for his contribution to this work.

Printed in U.S.A.

1

Constable Charlie Hobson was the first source of information all writers turned to if they were assigned a story on Eskimo. Charlie was what a modern Eskimo was all about. He was bright and reasonably good-looking. He had a college degree in law enforcement from the University of Oregon. He had a subscription to *National Geographic*, and Charlie hardly ever drank. Moreover, although thoroughly at home in the twentieth century, he was fiercely proud of his heritage.

In fact, when the five Eskimo communities formed a political alliance for the control of their destiny and lands, Charlie was one of the first to join them. He gave up his job with the Fairbanks Police Department. He sold his condo and his car, and moved up to Barrow to become the first semiofficial constable of the North Slope Borough. He rented a one-room modular apartment near the building that had once been Al's Cafe, got himself a red-carpeted office in the four-story Borough Administration building and proceeded to try and keep the peace.

In the beginning, when Barrow had been little more than a heap of shacks on the frozen tundra, law enforcement had been a fairly simple task. Three or four times a month an unhappy housewife stabbed her drunken husband or brother-in-law. Three or four times a week there were two-fisted brawls at the Polar Bear Bar and Grill. Once or twice a year a tribal feud ended in a shotgun blast, and the local boys were always stealing snowmobiles from the federal compound. But Charlie knew that with the discovery of oil and the money it brought, life in Barrow had changed—for the worse.

IT WAS A FRIDAY MORNING when what was left of Eddie Frank was discovered. Although spring had technically arrived two weeks earlier, the days remained gray with chilled fog banks, and the nights were filled with the moan of cracking ice as the warmer currents moved beneath. Daylight was appreciably longer, but the sun was still like a distant white wafer in the sky. And, although it had recently been unseasonably warm, the temperature had plunged well below freezing in the past twelve hours.

Charlie had only just got out of bed when Joey Upskin telephoned to say that Eddie had been found on the shore beyond Agiq Street. The wind, which had screamed through the town the night before, had finally died to a tolerable howl. But it was still too cold to venture outside without being completely prepared for it. So initially Charlie took his time. He switched on the hot plate and coaxed a stream of lukewarm water out of the shower head. He spent the usual five or six minutes trying to paste his thatch of coal-black hair in place, another three or four minutes rubbing salve into a sore on his lower lip. He then wolfed down two three-minute eggs and a bowl of cereal, topping it all off with a handful of Mega-vites. Then, finally slipping into his uniform, his boots and overcoat, Charlie picked up his side arm and moved out.

With nearly three thousand residents and a full-service department store, Barrow was no longer just another Eskimo village perched on the rim of the world. Moving through the streets, one found virtually every convenience available in Any Town, U.S.A.—including Chevy, Toyota, Subaru and Ford dealerships. Unfortunately the streets were also lined with the downside of modern prosperity: hulks of rusting washing machines, discarded sinks and radios, frozen sides of darkened meat and grids of gas and water lines.

It was only out beyond the end of Agiq Street that the landscape still resembled what Charlie's ancestors had found some four thousand years earlier: a place of deep silences and alternately of groaning ice. It was a place where the bears moved undisturbed in the evenings and the whales passed unseen in the mornings, and a body buried in the snow might well go undiscovered for a year.

The body lay across a snowdrift. From a distance, and peering through the iced windshield of his Jeep Cherokee, all Charlie saw was the stocky outline of Joey Upskin in a fur-trimmed parka and thermal boots. As he drew closer, he saw the huddled form of something lying at Joey's feet, something dark and shredded, like one of those discarded caribou carcasses.

Charlie eased the Cherokee to a stop below a low ridge and stepped out onto the frozen ground. Although there were greenish patches of lichen and moss, the landscape was mostly dun colored and barren to the pack-ice crush along the shore.

"You eat breakfast?" Upskin asked, approaching the Cherokee. "Because if you did, you may have to eat it all over again once you take a look at this."

At first all Charlie saw were the merest traces of blood, the hint that something had ripped through the skin of Eddie Frank's parka to expose a lining of wolverine fur. Then, moving closer through a shallow patch of frozen slush, he finally saw the man's face, his throat.

"First I think maybe his heart got him," Upskin said softly. "I think maybe he was out checking on the boat or something, and then all of a sudden his heart stops beating and he falls over dead."

Charlie took a deep breath of chilled air, then knelt and brushed away the wisps of ice and snow that had fallen on Eddie's throat. The throat had not been cut. It had been ripped. The flesh had been seized by some terrible force and then torn open with tremendous ferocity. There were also deep slashes along cheeks, and the left ear was missing.

"So then I think maybe it was ol' Mr. Polar Bear," Upskin continued softly. "I look at that hole in him, you know, and I think that maybe he had a little argument with ol' Mr. Polar Bear. Because sometimes the bear, he can get pretty pissed off at people."

Charlie rose to his feet again, shifting his gaze past the body to a line of wolf tracks in the dark, now-frozen soil. There were more traces of blood where the right rear paw had left an impression, and for a moment it crossed Charlie's mind that the animal must have been badly wounded because there were no impressions of the front paws. Then as a chill formed in the pit of his stomach, it struck him that there were no impressions of the front paws because the creature had been walking upright *like a man*!

"Who else have you told about this?" he asked.

Upskin shook his head. He was also staring at the tracks. "No one. I ain't told no one."

"And no one else has been out here? No one else could have seen this?"

Upskin shook his head, glancing back to the dark rows of ramshackle houses. "No one."

"Then let's make sure we keep it that way," Charlie said as he turned and walked back to his truck.

The two men got into the vehicle, but for a long time neither man spoke; their eyes remained fixed on the gray outline of the weathered shacks of Barrow. Now and again there were echos of a lonely snowmobile on the wind, but for the most part it remained very quiet.

"What do you know about them?" Charlie asked at last. "What do you know about the old stories?"

Upskin shook his head again and withdrew a flask of grain alcohol—190 proof. "Only what Granny Olive told me when I was a kid."

"And what was that?"

"That once upon a time there were some real powerful *anatqut*, which is what folks used to call the shamans. And some of these old shamans had the spirit of the wolf as their personal spirit-guide. Granny Olive called it their *tunarat*. And sometimes somebody or something made them mad enough, they would call their *tunarat* inside them so that they became wolves themselves. And then they took revenge on their enemies."

Charlie shut his eyes for a moment, his knuckles growing white around the steering wheel. "Did she ever say if any of those shamans were still around?"

Upskin shrugged, then took another slow pull from his flask. "She didn't say they were still around, but then again she didn't say they weren't. She just said that if you ever meet an old shaman who's got himself the spirit wolf as his *tunarat*, then you'd better run... which is what I'm going to do right now."

FOR A LONG TIME AFTER Upskin had tramped on back to the village, Charlie remained motionless in his seat. Although his left hand still rested on the steering wheel, his right hand now tightly gripped the butt of his Colt Python. Also in easy reach was a Marlin 336-CS rifle...as if any of the white man's weapons could stop an angry wolf that walked on two legs.

There were echoes of dogs barking from the village and the unearthly sound of more shifting ice in the bay. Then, suddenly bringing him back to the twentieth century, he heard the distant drone of the Atlantic Richfield plane en route to the oil fields at Prudhoe Bay.

Just stick to the facts, he told himself. Start thinking about the possibilities, and you'll go crazy. So just stick to the basic facts.

And yet what *were* the facts? he wondered as he shifted his gaze to the horribly twisted limbs of Eddie's torn body.

Eddie Frank had been a whaler, an old-fashioned, down-and-dirty bowhead whaler. Although he may have angered a few of the more progressive-minded villagers with his talk about maintaining the natural balance of things, everyone had basically liked him. Some had even looked up to the man, respected him as one of the last real traditionalists. So then why had he been butchered? And more to the point, by what? This had not been done by a bear.

There were sounds of a radio on the wind, snatches of a song called "Welcome to the Jungle." Then Charlie heard the sound of dogs crying for their breakfast and another throbbing engine. He had to hide the body, he quickly told himself. He had to cover the tracks and get the body out of sight before the whole village started to panic. He knew that something like this could not be kept secret for long, not in a place as small as Barrow, but he felt better just having decided on a course of action.

Charlie eased open the door of the Cherokee, stepped back onto the chilled ground and slowly walked around to the tailgate of the truck. After rummaging through an old box of road flares and thermal blankets, he finally withdrew a rubberized body bag generally used to collect dead animals from the roadside. Jamming the bag under his left arm and a short-handled shovel under his right, he moved out toward the body. Although the wind had grown marginally weaker, the air remained dead cold.

Because the arms and legs had been frozen at an awkward angle, he did not even attempt to encase the body in the bag. He simply laid the rubberized sheet over the remains, then secured the ends as best he could. Later, one of the boys from the medical center could figure out how to pry Eddie out of the frosted earth and fit him into the back of a truck. For the moment, however, it was enough to cover him.

Charlie hesitated before picking up the shovel to cover the tracks. He tried to calculate the size of the creature that had left those paw prints. Although not an experienced hunter, he knew that the beast must have weighed at least a hundred and fifty pounds. He was also fairly certain that the thing had been tall, at least as tall as a man.

He worked quickly, almost feverishly, scraping at the meager soil to remove every trace of the prints. Although it would be obvious to any casual observer that someone had gone to a lot of trouble to hide something, he didn't care. He cared only that those tracks were obliterated, that the telltale prints of a wolf that walked on two legs were gone.

When he had finished the job, he dropped to one knee and slowly scanned the ground around him. Yes, there would be questions. And yes, there would be talk. But in the end, people would have no choice but to accept his explanation. Having wandered out in the night to secure his supplies from the wind, Eddie Frank had dropped dead of a heart attack. As for the wounds—well, obviously one of the village dogs had gnawed on the corpse.

Reasonably satisfied that he had at least bought himself some time, he rose to his feet and started tramping back to the vehicle. As he passed the body, he took another quick glance at the grotesque form beneath the rubberized bag. But having fixed the explanation very firmly in his mind, he was no longer afraid....

Or at least not until he heard the howl of the wolf, high and clear above the wind.

2

It was just after dawn, and Carl "Ironman" Lyons had been tracking a bull moose for more than two hours. Finally drawing in range of his quarry along the spine of a wooded hill, he had suddenly found himself transfixed by the high and clear call of the wolves.

It was his third day along the peninsula outside Anchorage. Five days earlier he and the other members of Able Team had spent sixteen hours tracking a number of cocaine cowboys to the wilds of Los Angeles. Given that LAPD had not been too happy about the ensuing bloodshed and that the Drug Enforcement Agency had not been overly thrilled about losing a witness, it was decided that Able Team should take a little vacation. Stalking moose in the bush outside Anchorage had seemed like a pretty good idea at the time.

Carl Lyons, a former cop with LAPD and now a valued member of America's toughest antiterrorist squad, lay down his Weatherby Mark V Magnum and picked up his field glasses. As far as he could tell, there were three wolves watching from the high ground: two females and a magnificent gray male. When he had first caught sight of the wolves, he hadn't paid them much attention. He was stalking a moose, and everything else had seemed irrelevant. Then, ascending through the long shadows of the pines to the rise of the hill, he had actually come face-to-face with that old gray wolf.

And the beast had looked right through him...jaws slack, head cocked, eyes locked on his eyes as if to say: You may be a great hunter in the cities, but here I'm the great hunter. Stand clear, because the moose is mine. There had been at least two opportunities to bag the moose after that encounter, but Lyons could only watch.

He continued watching until the wolves had encircled the animal, until he was certain that the moose was doomed. Then, because he sensed that their kill was a private act, he picked up his gear and started back through the pines to the camp. Thirty yards below the ridge, he thought he heard the animal's death call. But given the cries of surrounding crows, he couldn't be sure.

IT WAS FULLY LIGHT by the time Lyons returned to the camp. Hermann "Gadgets" Schwarz, Able Team's electronics wizard, was huddled over a camp stove, attempting to brew a pot of coffee. Beside him, and still shivering from the frigid night, sat Rosario "Pol" Blancanales, the Team's wiry special weapons man and covert operative. Pol was talking to Danny Skagway, local tracker from the Tlingit tribe, who went everywhere with his dog, Flash. There were odors of burnt bacon, the fresh scent of the pines and kerosene.

"So, Dawn Tracker," Schwarz smirked as Lyons drew closer, "where's the antlers?"

"In his pocket." Blancanales smiled.

Lyons started to reply in kind, but suddenly recalled the cry of those wolves. He simply shrugged. "The antlers are where they belong," he said. "On the moose."

He poured himself a cup of coffee, added a spoonful of powdered milk and then squatted down beside Skagway.

Although the stocky Indian had not been told exactly who his clients were, nor what they did for a living, he had sensed from the start that Lyons and company were not the usual urban sportsmen up for a weekend kill. The way they moved through the forest and the way they handled their firearms had been a dead giveaway. And now, squatting beside the lanky blond Lyons, who gazed out toward the high pines, he sensed it in the man's voice.

"Tell me about the wolves," Lyons said, his voice flat and dry, his gaze remaining fixed on the distance.

"The wolves?" Skagway replied.

Lyons nodded to the high ground, to the spine of the hill where he and the wolf had first locked eyes. "Up there. The pack that runs with the old gray one."

Skagway began thoughtfully chewing on his lower lip, then finally responded with a slow nod. "Yeah," he finally breathed. "I know those wolves."

"So what's their story?"

Skagway shrugged. "The old one, he's called Proud Tooth. The others, those are his wives and his brothers. I don't think anyone knows where they came from, but usually in the spring they come down from the mountains for the moose, and sometimes for the Dall sheep."

"Do you think you can get me close enough to shoot them?"

Skagway turned with a tight frown. Before he could speak, however, Lyons withdrew a 35 mm camera and long-range lens from his backpack. "With this. I want to shoot them with this."

THEY WAITED until the late afternoon before finally moving out to the high ground. Although there were no longer any audible cries from the wolves, Skagway explained that the pack was still out there—resting among the deeper glades, maybe gnawing on the carcass of the moose. As they passed beyond the pines and on to the rocky slopes, Schwarz and Blancanales began complaining about the photographic mission. But when they finally caught sight of the enormous gray beast, perched on the rocky slope above the trailhead, they all fell strangely silent.

"So that's your wolf, huh?" Blancanales said softly, peering up a hundred feet to the stark outline of the beast on the ridge.

"Yeah," Lyons breathed. "That's my wolf."

"And all you want to do is take a picture of him?"

"Yeah, I just want to take a picture."

Blancanales squinted back up through the fading light to the outline of the wolf on the ridge, its fur suddenly more silver than gray, its massive shoulders hunched and its head cocked in anticipation. "Well, I can understand that," Blancanales finally said.

From the base of the ridge, Skagway led them to a copse of deep ferns in the shadows of the steeper slope. Here and there among the pines were small patches of snow, but most of the ground was dry and barren.

"He knows we're here," Skagway whispered, "but I think he's going to let you take his picture. I think he senses your strength."

"So how do we get closer?" Lyons asked.

"Slowly." The Indian smiled. "Very slowly."

From the ferns, they followed a deer path to a small plateau just below the ridge. Although by no means a professional photographer, Lyons had decided that his wolf would best be shot against the setting sun. He had also decided that he would like to get a photograph of the animal on the move, maybe running with the others along the spine of the hill.

But before he could even draw close enough to fix a range, the animal suddenly bolted at the clatter of an incoming chopper.

Skagway reacted first, shouting something over his shoulder and then breaking into a sprint. Beyond him, and still not certain what was happening, Lyons also broke into a run. As he neared the top of the hill, he heard Blancanales shout, "Will somebody please tell me what the hell is going on?" But by then the chopper had risen above the ridge and it was obvious what was going on.

Lyons turned and watched the wolves run hard as the helicopter descended from out of the sun. They ran for the low ground and the shadows of the pines. For a moment the Able Team warrior was fairly certain that the wolves were going to make it. But then he saw the rifleman lean from the open cockpit, saw the long barrel of the Winchester M-70 swing into play and the glint of light off the scope.

Skagway shouted something else as the echo of the first shot rolled out of the sky, something in his native tongue. Then came the second and third shots, and he simply sank to his knees.

The first wolf, a lean female, dropped with a pitiful yelp. When her hind legs gave out, she managed to drag herself another fifteen feet before finally slipping into the grass. Arching with the impact of a second shot to the spine, she then shuddered and lay still.

The second wolf, also a female, seemed to leap before she fell, a high, almost playful, leap that left her in a trembling heap. Although the old gray male must have obviously sensed that death was near, he hesitated, glancing longingly at his mates.

A lot of things went through Carl Lyons's mind as he watched the chopper circle in the sky. He thought about what he had felt when he'd come upon the wolf and when he'd gazed into his eyes. He thought about killing that sadistic coke freak in Los Angeles, laying four slugs into the windshield of a speeding car and watching the animal's head explode. Then he thought about what the female must have felt when that Winchester Magnum shattered her spine and what the male must have felt as he watched....

And without even really thinking, he unslung his Weatherby, rammed a slug into the chamber and sighted up at the chopper.

He heard Schwarz calling his name from the rise of the hill, and Blancanales shouting, "Carl, it's not worth it." He also heard Skagway shouting his name.

But he ignored them all as he finally sighted on the rifleman. He saw the bulky form through the glinting Plexiglas, saw the tanned face pressed to the stock of the Winchester. Then he felt the muscles in his neck contract and the hatred rise from the pit of his stomach like a sudden wash of vomit.

"You animal," he whispered as the rifleman eased the Winchester into line with the old gray wolf.

But even as Lyons felt the pressure of his finger on the trigger, he knew that he couldn't possibly fire, couldn't possibly kill a man over a wolf. So in the end he simply screamed, screamed out in obscene rage as the Winchester kicked in the rifleman's arms and the old gray shuddered with the impact of a slug in his brain.

The wolf fell about fifteen yards from his mates. Although the left side of his head had been shattered, he almost looked as if he was sleeping. His eyes were shut and his jaws were slack to reveal the tip of the faintly pink tongue. The breeze gently rippling through the fur revealed a myriad of subtle colors that had not been obvious at a distance.

"If you want me to help you bury them..." Blancanales said as he came up behind Lyons. "If you want me to..." He broke off when he realized that his friend wasn't even listening.

For a moment no one said anything, while Lyons and Skagway simply stared at the wolves.

"So who were they?" Lyons finally asked. "Those guys in the chopper, who were they?"

Skagway shrugged, glancing up to the now silent sky. "I don't know," he breathed. "They could have been anyone. Maybe lawyers from San Francisco. Maybe doctors from Chicago. Maybe even oilmen from Prudhoe Bay."

"And why do they do it? I mean what's the sport in shooting something from a chopper?"

Skagway shrugged again. "I guess you'll have to ask them that question."

"Yeah, well, maybe I'll just do that," Lyons sighed as he took a last look at the wolf.

3

"Are you going to tell me what's going on, or are we going to keep playing Twenty Questions?"

Dr. Lippman faced Charlie Hobson from across the table on which Eddie Frank's body now lay. He was a tall, thin man with dark eyes and rimless glasses. According to local rumor, he had originally come to Barrow in order to escape a malpractice suit and paying seven thousand dollars a month in alimony. Some also claimed that his real name was Watson and that he had killed a man on the operating table in Detroit. But then they claimed that virtually every white man in Barrow was running from something.

"So how about it, Charlie?" the doctor persisted. "Are you going to tell me the truth or not?"

Charlie responded with an awkward grin. "What's wrong, Doc, you don't like my report?"

The doctor shrugged. "Oh, I like it just fine—as a piece of fiction," he said, slowly drawing back the bloody sheet that had been draped across Frank's corpse. "Now, I ain't exactly a trained coroner, but I know a heart-attack victim when I see one, and this man did not die of a bad heart. Just take a look at this clotting—there's no way it was caused by a heart attack."

Charlie slumped across the doorjamb, casually letting his gaze wander across the blue-green walls of the Barrow Medical Center. "Okay, then you tell me," he finally said. "Uh, what did he die of?"

Lippman passed a hand, clad in a surgical glove, over the gaping throat wound. "This missing piece of throat right here. That's what killed him."

The sheet was drawn back over the body, and the doctor stepped away from the stainless-steel table.

"Now, I ain't going to tell you how to do your job," Lippman continued after a long silence. "But the fact is, Charlie-boy, this here Eskimo didn't die of natural causes. Maybe some sort animal got him, or maybe some sort of person who wanted to make it look like an animal killed him. But either way, you've got yourself a murder on your hands, and that's all there is to it."

Charlie finally just nodded and moved back out through the dingy corridors to the cold streets of Barrow.

THREE DAYS PASSED, three days of wary glances and unspoken suspicions. Although no one specifically talked about Eddie Frank's death in terms of ancient and terrible powers, it was obvious that everyone sensed powerful forces were involved. It was in the eyes of the children and in the whispers of the men hunched over coffee in Mike's Cafe. It was in the silence and the stillness of the nights.

Charlie stood at the grimy window of his apartment, a bottle of Jack Daniel's at his elbow. Earlier that afternoon he had briefly toyed with the idea of driving out to the western shacks to question some of Eddie's friends—the crew of his whaler, for example, or the girl who use to clean his quarters. But then, when searching for a box of wadcutters in his closet, he'd found an old dog-eared book he'd picked up in Fairbanks: *The Way of the Two-Legged Wolf*. Quickly leafing through the index, he'd come to a passage on the shaman.

He went over the information that he'd read once again, but his thoughts were interrupted when his eyes registered the arrival of a Chevy Blazer.

He recognized the driver the moment she stepped out of the vehicle— Miss Maggie Defoe from the Environmental Protection Agency. She was a bleeding-heart liberal, an Eskimo lover and a staunch opponent of anything that smacked of progress. She was also not bad to look at, for a skinny white girl. Although she spent most of her time at Prudhoe Bay, he had seen her around many times, taking ice samples out on the northern floe, questioning the whalers and the sealers, examining the carcasses of their kills. He also knew that despite her shaggy mane of straw-blond hair and her freckles, she was a no-nonsense type of person, and that this was no social call.

Charlie greeted her from the doorway, offering a silent nod and as friendly a smile as he could muster. She replied with an equally curt nod, then followed him up the sagging wooden staircase and into his dreary apartment. "So what brings the EPA all the way out here?" he asked cheerfully as he placed a pot of water on the hot plate.

But the answer was obvious from the look in her eyes and the way she examined the book on his table.

Charlie cleared her a seat on his worn sofa and then tossed another caribou chip into the stove. He thought about offering her a shot of Jack Daniel's, but finally decided that she might not think it professional. He knew that he'd already had more than enough to drink that afternoon.

"It's about Eddie Frank," she said after a long moment's silence. "It's about what I think really happened to him, and why."

He turned to face her from the doorway of his tiny kitchen. "Do you mind if I ask you something, Miss Defoe? I mean, before we both end up saying things we might regret."

She glanced at the bottle of Jack Daniel's on the windowsill, then back to the book on the table. "You can ask me anything you want, just so long as it's a two-way street."

"All right, then tell me this. Did you come here in an *official* capacity, or did Eddie Frank just happen to be a friend?"

She glanced at the shotgun in the corner and back to the box of wadcutters on the coffee table. "And if I were to say that it's official?"

"Then I'd have to tell you that Eddie Frank died of a heart attack."

She rose from the couch to examine a tiny carving of a killer whale cut from the tusk of a walrus. "You never really lived out on the ice, did you, Constable? Never lived out there like your ancestors, eating only what you could kill by means of weapons that you fashioned with your hands."

"What's that got to do with anything?"

"What do you think?" she asked, suddenly turning to face him. "Look, why don't we stop playing games with one another? Why don't we just talk about what really happened to Eddie Frank?"

He reached for the Jack Daniel's, no longer caring how it looked or what she thought. "All right, lady, you want to talk about what really happened to Eddie Frank? We'll talk about what really happened to Eddie Frank. But I just want you to know that officially I'm not changing my report for anyone—not for you, not for your so-called Environmental Protection Agency, not for anybody. Officially Eddie dropped dead from a bad heart, and while he was laying out there on the ice, one of the village dogs took a few bites out of him, and that's all there is to say about it."

"Except, of course, that it wasn't a dog that took that bite out of the man's throat," she said softly. "It was a certain strange variety of wolf. And Eddie wasn't dead when it attacked him. He was as alive as you and I."

She moved to the window, still toying with that carving. "Look, I don't pretend to know what it's like to have Eskimo blood in my veins, to know what it feels like to stand on the floe with a whaling harpoon in my hands. But I do know one or two things about fear, about the kind of fear that you never outgrow no matter how far removed you become from your past."

"Eskimo people are not ignorant savages, Miss Defoe. We are business people, people who own property, people who run factories, people who make laws and even collect taxes from oil companies."

"But at the same time they are also people who still have a fear of the shamans, and you know it."

She turned from the window to face him again. "I'd like to tell you my theory about what happened to Eddie Frank. It may not be exactly what's going on, but I think it's pretty close. Whoever killed Eddie Frank didn't do it simply because he happened to be out on the ice that night. He was killed for a specific reason, a reason that hits right at the core of this community and the Eskimo people. It may appear that his murderer was a monster, but that's only because the killer wants us to believe that. He wants us to think in terms of half-remembered myths and supernatural powers. But Eddie's killer was real—he was not based in any myth."

Charlie sank to the armchair that he had won in the All Eskimo Lottery. They had also given him a trophy, but it had broke in the quake of '64. "How do you know all this?" he finally asked. "How do you even know what happened to Eddie?"

She looked at him again. "Does it matter?" she asked as she sat back down on the couch. "Look at it this way, Constable. What kind of a man was Eddie? Yes, he was a whaler, but he was also an environmentalist. He stood for restricted land access and drilling rights. He stood for the whaling tradition, for hunting with harpoons instead of bombs, for taking only what one needs rather than what one wants. In short, he stood for everything that the oil companies do not. And most important of all, people listened to him. They respected him. And when he said that Eskimo lands should not be invaded by oil companies, that counted for something."

Charlie ran his hand across his mouth, then slowly took a deep breath. "So why would they have made it look like a shaman killing? Huh? Answer me that? Why didn't they just shoot the poor bastard?"

"Because they wanted to make an example of him, and because they wanted to instill a sense of fear throughout the community. Because of the way he died, they probably hoped we would chalk his death up to a tribal feud."

Charlie shook his head. "You know the Eskimo word for ghost, lady? *Ilitkosiq*. Well, that's what you're doing. You're chasing *ilitkosiq*. You got some idea in your head that all the oil companies are bad and now you're chasing ghosts."

"I don't think so, Charlie. I think the only ghost out there is Eddie Frank's, and I think he was murdered because he was speaking out against the offshore exploration program."

"And what's so bad about that program? Don't you think Eskimo need money, too? Don't you think that maybe hunting and fishing is for the birds and that maybe we'd like to be oil tycoons for a while, too?"

"What I think, Charlie, is unimportant. All that's important is that somebody murdered Eddie Frank, and I can prove it."

He lifted his eyes from the filthy purple shag carpet, and finally met her gaze head-on. "What do you mean you can prove it?"

"Eddie Frank had some friends at Prudhoe Bay, people from this community who had access to certain oil company documents."

He gave her a sideways glance. "What kind of documents?"

"Documents that outline exactly what I've been talking about—a plan to divide and conquer the Eskimo community by exploiting the old superstitions."

"And he gave you those documents?"

"Not exactly, but I know where they are." She rose to her feet, still gazing directly into his eyes. "So how about it, Constable? You want to find out what really happened to Eddie Frank, or do you want to just keep staring at the walls with a bottle of whiskey in your hand?''

4

All was in flux beyond the frozen mantle of the shoreline. Old ice, retreating with the spring swells, collided with the new to form jagged walls of frozen rubble. Mile-long sheets of floating ice surged into pressure ridges, gouging out deep trenches from the silt below. Drifting floes, jostled together, submerged and then rose again.

To be an Eskimo is to know the ice.

For fifteen minutes Maggie Defoe and Charlie Hobson drove in silence, listening and watching as slow-shifting ice groaned beyond the edge of the Barrow shore. At one point Charlie had offered Miss Defoe a wedge of dried gum scraped from the jaw of a bowhead whale. He'd also tapped on the windshield of the Cherokee to draw her attention to the spectacular view of the cracking mantle. For a long time, however, neither spoke.

Finally, pointing to what looked like a hillock of filthy snow on the shore, Maggie told Charlie to ease his foot off the accelerator.

"I think he called it his *tawvsliq*," she said as they drew closer to the dwelling of dun-colored sod.

"That's right," Charlie said. "We call it a *tawvsliq*."

"He said that he wanted to get back to his roots, to live like his grandfather lived. So he built himself a sod house according to the old plan."

"And you think that's where he was headed when... when I found him?"

"Yeah," Maggie sighed. "I think that's where he was headed."

Charlie cut the engine and coasted the last fifty feet to a stop. Basically a domed dwelling with an oblong passage from the surface, it was actually built into the ground rather than on top of it. In addition to the side windows, there was a skylight of stretched walrus bladder. Although outwardly crude, the dwelling could keep up to ten people and a dozen dogs comfortably warm and safe from even the worst Arctic storms. Isolated and deserted in the dead of the evening, however, it seemed very forboding.

"He used to come out here when he wanted to be alone," Maggie said when they had stepped out of the Cherokee. "He used to come here to listen to the wind and the ice."

Although there were tire tracks near the entrance of the *tawvsliq* and scattered rifle shells along the frozen track, the sod house might have been built five thousand years ago. The central frame consisted of four upright posts, connected at the top by willow withes. In the center, and away from the direction of the prevailing wind, were the two heavier posts of the door frame. Then came the low passageway, sealed with scraped skins and sod. It led to the living quarters.

Charlie and Maggie hesitated at the entrance, examining the ground for fresh tracks. In keeping with the old ways, Eddie Frank had tied amulets to the door frame: a stuffed lemming, a chain of polar bear teeth, a wolf's paw.

"Tell me something," Charlie said softly. They were squatting side by side at the door frame, peering past the shaved skins into the darkened passage. "How come Eddie told you about this place?"

She fingered the chain of polar bear teeth. "You mean how come he trusted a white girl with his secrets?" She smiled.

"Yeah. How come he trusted a white girl?"

She gently drew the door skin aside and slipped into the gloom. "Because he knew that I cared about this way of life."

The passageway was spacious, with storage alcoves cut into the smooth sod walls and a sleeping alcove for guests. Beyond the alcoves, two whale skulls had been wedged into the permafrost to serve as steps and to help support the central frames. There was also an ornamental walrus skull and another piece of dried walrus intestine across the frontal skylight. Beyond the passage lay a sunken entrance well where the women had traditionally stood when cooking. Next, there was the raised sod *iga* and smoke hole for the fire, and finally the larders for the storage and thawing of meat.

"I guess you might say Eddie straddled the centuries," Maggie whispered as she crouched beside Hobson to examine a cellular phone and battery pack. "One foot in the twentieth, and one foot in the first." Also on the ledge at the end of the passage was a Remington Lightweight fitted with an Aimpoint electronic sight.

"And what was the deal with the documents?" Charlie asked, shifting his gaze from the high-tech gear to the primitive slope of the sod walls.

Maggie shook her head. "I don't know the whole story. I only know that Eddie had a contact at Prudhoe Bay, one of the village boys who worked on the drills. Apparently when this boy saw a copy of the memo outlining the consortium's plans to end the offshore drilling protest, he knew immediately that it was just the proof Eddie had been looking for."

"So this kid stole the memo from the administrative offices and passed it on to Eddie."

"Something like that, yeah."

"So where is it?"

She shook her head again, scanning the dim interior of the dwelling. "Where would an Eskimo hide a secret that could kill him?"

THEY SPENT about twenty minutes probing the smooth sod walls before Maggie discovered the irregular chink below a planked alcove. Using a pocketknife and a flashlight, she finally withdrew an oilskin packet the size of a legal envelope. The ends of the packet had been carefully stitched with greased thread and sealed with candle wax. A crude drawing of a bearded seal had been scratched into the oilskin with a needle, while a fox's tooth had been sewn into the stitching for luck.

"Maybe we'd better talk about the ground rules," Maggie said. "About what we're going to do with these papers and how we're going to do it."

They were seated side by side on the low sod bench that filled the center of the dwelling. The packet lay between them, still unopened.

Charlie extended a hand and began gently tugging at the thread. "The ground rules are simple," he said.

"These are stolen documents in my jurisdiction, and I decide what we do with them."

She laid her hand on the packet. "No deal, Constable. These documents are going to keep your people from losing their heritage, and we're going to use them as I see fit."

Charlie met the girl's eyes for a moment, the loose thread still coiled around his index finger. Finally nodding with a small smile, he said, "All right, lady, we'll do it your way. But how about we see exactly what we got here, huh?"

Maggie picked up the Swiss Army knife and quickly cut the tight knots of greased thread. Charlie had switched on the flashlight in order to illuminate her work as she tore away the folds of the oilskin. But before actually withdrawing the wad of typewritten papers, she hesitated, head cocked, listening.

There was a low moan of wind across the hard ice, then the deeper rumble of what might have been a truck.

"What's that?" she asked softly.

Charlie glanced up to the skylight. "What's what?"

The wind seemed to die as the truck drew to a stop.

"That!"

Charlie rose to a crouch and withdrew his Colt Python from the holster. "You tell anyone we're coming here today?" he whispered.

She shook her head with a quick smirk. "What do you think?"

"All right, then wait here."

There were sounds of footsteps just beyond the sod wall. Charlie paused at the entrance well, peering into the gloom at the end of the passage. Then, hearing what might have been another tentative step on the hard ground beyond the walls, he slowly inched forward to the first row of support posts.

From where Maggie sat, still huddled on the sod bench, there was a moment when it seemed as if he had discovered the source of the footsteps and had determined that there was nothing to worry about. For a moment Charlie even seemed to smile and shake his head.

Then, without warning, it was on him: a furious form had crashed through the skylight in a flurry of gray fur and clung to Charlie's back.

Maggie caught a glimpse of the snapping jaws, then heard herself scream as bright blood splattered across the ceiling. She caught a second glimpse of the creature's face, the long snout and the coal-black eyes. She saw Charlie struggling to throw the creature from his back, then saw him as another bright explosion of blood burst from his throat.

"Run!" she heard him shout. "For God's sake, run!"

There were echoes of a cracking bone as he began thrashing with agonized screams, then the terrible click-click of those snapping jaws. Maggie screamed again as she watched, paralyzed at the vision of a lupine form ripping and tearing on two legs.

This is real, she thought vaguely, still too stunned to move. This is really happening, and I've got to get out of here!

But even before she could drag herself to her feet, the creature's eyes were leveled on her. Slowly rising from Charlie's mangled body, it started toward her through the darkened passage.

She glanced at the Remington on the planked shelf, quickly calculated the distance and decided that she'd never make it. She fingered the pocketknife in her left hand, but knew it would be useless. Then, finally rising to her haunches and meeting the creature's gaze again, she sprang for the window behind her.

She tore away the stretched intestine that served as the window's covering and plunged headlong through the narrow passageway into the evening chill. She felt a hand or a claw close around her ankle like a steel vise, but managed to kick it off. Maggie caught another glance of the creature's face as she scrambled across the slippery ground to the constable's Cherokee, then saw the thing again as she slid behind the wheel and turned the ignition key.

But when she finally shifted into gear and tromped down hard on the accelerator, she was conscious of nothing except a wild smear of impressions: the gray form of an upright beast leaping to avoid the swerving jeep, the Cherokee's engine screaming above the scream of the creature, the tires briefly skidding on frozen earth before finally catching hold and propelling her to safety.

Eventually it also passed through her mind, with a dull ache, that she no longer had that packet of documents, that it must have slipped out of her hands when she scrambled through the window. But by the time she realized this, she had already traveled some fifteen miles across the frozen landscape.

MAGGIE DEFOE EVENTUALLY found refuge at a vacant military outpost just north of Wainwright. There, after coaxing a fire from Sterno cans and a heap of yellowed newspapers, she managed to radio the EPA office in Nome. Nome, in turn, put her on to the Washington office, and by midnight—eastern standard time—all sorts of whispered telephone calls had been made, including a particularly discreet call to one Hal Brognola, operational head of Stony Man Farm in Virginia. Brognola, in turn, placed a call to Anchorage.

5

It was just after seven in the morning when Carl Lyons received the telephone call from Hal Brognola. Typically Brognola's message was cryptic and terse. There was a problem in the north, Brognola said. The solution was possibly nonnegotiable and therefore Lyons was advised to take special equipment.

"Just how far north are you talking?" Lyons asked, gazing through a sooty motel window to a bleak and gray skyline.

"Let's just say that you'd better make damn sure you take your mittens," Brognola replied.

"And is there any way you can give me an idea what this involves?"

Brognola hesitated before responding, and Lyons had a clear vision of the man seated at his desk, chomping on his ever-present cigar. "Let me put it like this," Brognola said after a long silence. "The underlying issue could not be much blacker. You understand me?"

"Yeah," Lyons answered. "I understand."

"Then I suppose I don't have to tell you that the overall problem might also get a little sticky."

"No, you don't have to tell me that."

"So stay alert, but stay cool."

Two minutes later, complaining that the phone had woken him, Pol Blancanales entered from the adjoining room. Behind him, still in his shorts and undershirt, stood a sleepy Gadgets Schwarz.

"So?" Blancanales asked.

"So we're going to the Arctic to handle a little problem regarding oil," Lyons said. Able Team—the nation's hard-hitting covert action squad—was back in business.

PREPARATIONS BEGAN that morning. In addition to the modified .45 autos that the team habitually carried into action, Lyons managed to procure three Marlin 336-CS deer rifles equipped with 12x Redfield scopes. He would have preferred something fully automatic and with more flexibility, such as the MP-5, but one had to take what one could get in the field. Next came the clothing: thermal socks and underwear, Pendleton shirts, insulated rubber boots, face masks, snow packs and maximum-strength Arctic parkas.

Able Team was able to catch an afternoon Wien Air Alaska flight to Nome. From Nome they caught a six-seater that flew over Brooks Range and beyond the Gates of the Arctic. Upon reaching the narrow strip at Barrow, they were met by a sullen native driver in a new but already battered Toyota. Without asking where his passengers wished to be taken, the driver proceeded to the Sheffield Hotel on the westward end of Agiq Street—one hundred and fifty-six dollars a night for a single, no discounts, no exceptions. The lobby was filled with locals, mostly Eskimo teenagers with nothing to do and no place to go. After securing two rooms with a view of corrugated rooftops and the shore-fast ice, Lyons led the team into the streets in search of something to eat. Although the sky was clear, the air was like a knife, and everywhere the locals stared in hostile silence.

Upon returning to the hotel with the first chill of the evening at their backs, Lyons and company found a fifteen or sixteen-year-old Eskimo boy squatting on the filthy shag outside the door of one of their hotel rooms. The boy wore a ragged Washington State University sweatshirt under his parka and a black elastic headband. As Lyons drew closer, the kid rose to his feet and nodded. Lyons responded with an equally careful nod and ushered the kid inside.

"I'm just the messenger, okay?" the boy said nervously.

"Then how about giving us your message?" Schwarz said from the corner of the room.

The boy took a deep breath and then nodded again. "I'm just here to tell you that the EPA lady is waiting for you, that she's waiting for you and I'm going to take you to her."

"Waiting where?" Blancanales asked.

The boy nodded to the window, to the long view of the shore-fast ice and the yellow-brown tundra beyond. "Out there."

Lyons studied the boy, glancing at his T-shirt, his insulated running shoes and finally his eyes. "All right," he said. "You take us to her."

Ten minutes later, after climbing into the boy's rusting Honda Accord, Able Team moved out east across the unpaved tundra roads. Once or twice, above the rattle of the engine and the echo of the wind across the ice sheets, Lyons thought he might have heard the cries of wolves… But it may have just been the screech of metal cranes from the oil fields.

6

There were dozens of facilities across the Arctic similar to the one where Miss Defoe waited: a small complex of insulated Quonset huts, a radio tower and a storage shed. Originally built in the fifties as part of the string of Early Warning outposts, the structure had been left to rot more than two decades ago. But because nothing really rots in the Arctic, it simply continued to sit. In all, there were four Quonset huts at the outpost: a storage shed where she had left the vehicle beside an old All Terrain Vehicle, an abandoned radio room, and the sleeping quarters.

It was half-past seven when Lyons and the others reached the facility. The Eskimo boy, who had finally told them his name was Ronnie, pulled his Honda into the long shadows of the radio tower but left the engine running against the cold. Then, without turning around, without even glancing at his passengers, he announced that this was the end of the line.

"Does that mean you're not waiting?" Schwarz asked from the cramped rear seat.

The boy shrugged. "I wait, something goes wrong, then what? Eskimo boy like me could get in a lot of trouble out here. Besides, she's got the constable's Jeep *and* this real cherry ATV. You know, an All Terrain Vehicle?"

Schwarz cleared a visible circle in the frosted rear window and peered out to the road that faded into the fog, the treeless horizon and the frozen shore. "Yeah, well that makes me feel a whole better," he sighed. "A whole lot better."

After collecting their bags from the rear of the Honda, Lyons and his team moved out across the semi-frozen path toward the Quonset huts. They had not quite reached the chain-link fence when the Honda pulled away and left them in silence. For a moment there was only the sound of the wind through the wires and their footsteps on the tundra.

They heard Maggie Defoe before they saw her—a thin, frightened voice from deep within the corrugated structure: "I've got a shotgun, and you're all in my range!"

Lyons exchanged a wary glance with Schwarz and Blancanales, then cupped his gloved hand to his mouth. "Well, good for you, lady. Now, how about letting us come inside before we freeze our butts off?"

"First tell me who sent you."

Lyons and the others exchanged another quick glance before Ironman brought his gloved hand to his mouth again. "Do the words 'Stony Man' mean anything to you?"

They heard the sound of a sliding bolt, the squeal of runners on cold metal, and finally they saw Maggie Defoe.

"Sorry about that," she said. "But I had to be certain that Ronnie had picked up the right people."

She was standing in the darkened doorway of the Quonset. In a powder-blue parka and thermal trousers, she looked vaguely like an Eskimo girl, except for the wisps of blond hair and freckles.

The hut was long and low, a stark reminder that life in this wilderness had never been particularly comfortable. Aided by the faint glow of kerosene lamps, they took in the abandoned clutter of a distant military outpost: a row of sagging cots, a cheap stereo, heaps of pornographic magazines, a block of gray-green government filing cabinets and a chipped steel desk. It was, however, reasonably warm once the door was sealed again.

"The problem is that we didn't really have a description of you," Maggie Defoe continued as she led her guests inside. "And even if we had had one, most white people look the same to Eskimo."

"Well, why don't you just tell us exactly who it was you thought we might be?" Lyons said, laying down his weapons' bag and slipping out of his parka.

She moved to a warped steel cabinet and withdrew a bottle of Wild Turkey. "I'm not sure," she replied. "That's part of the problem. I'm just not sure."

They settled on the cots, sipping the drink from battered tin cups. The wind sounded very loud through the loose plates of sheeting on the roof, and occasionally there were echoes of cracking ice along the shoreline. But when Maggie finally began to talk, it suddenly seemed very quiet.

"I guess you could look at this two ways," she said. "I suppose on the one hand you could say that this involves certain native forces that are almost as old as that ice out there. It is also a problem of the future, of how we're going to manage this land and this environment."

"Now you're talking about oil," Lyons said softly. "That right?"

She took another sip and nodded. "Yeah, I'm talking about oil. You see, for about five years now, geologists have been speculating on just how much oil lies off the North Slope shore. Naturally estimates vary, but the fact is there may be more than sixty billion dollars worth of oil under that ice. Sixty billion."

"But the Eskimo don't want it drilled, is that it?" Blancanales asked.

She shook her head. "Not necessarily. I mean, after all, when you're talking sixty billion dollars, you're talking a language that anyone can understand—even the most traditional elements of the native community. But there are some, mostly the old-timers and a few younger whalers, who don't give a damn about the money, not if it means destroying their ancestral lands."

"And Eddie Frank was one of those who opposed the drilling?" Blancanales assumed.

"That's right," she said.

A nautical map of the North Slope and surrounding sea was laid on a cot, the corners secured with paperback books and an ashtray.

"If you believe the geological surveys," Maggie began, "the most promising drilling sites are along this stretch. And if you listen to the oil companies, extraction would be a pretty straightforward process. They say they can drill from either artificial islands dredged up from the bottom, or drill directionally from the shore. There's also been talk of drilling from ships that could detach themselves from the pipes if and when the ice starts moving. But the problem isn't just the ebb and flow of ice. The problem is what the Eskimo call *ivu*."

A second map was withdrawn, a gray-and-white polar view of the Arctic Circle. There were a number of penciled mathematical calculations along the margins and several bold slashes in red crayon across the ice slabs.

"Technically, *ivu* is what you might call an extreme condition," Maggie continued. "It's a sudden shift of ice sheets, one on top of another. The result is a kind of a chain reaction producing an absolutely incredible amount of pressure. I talked to one village elder who told me that he once saw the ice packs surge across the shoreline with such force that in a matter of minutes the coast was buried beneath frozen waves, some of them fifty to seventy feet high. Now, you take that kind of natural possibility and factor in four or five offshore drilling sites, and you could wind up with one hell of a problem. You could wind up with an ice sheet moving in and severing a pipe before anyone can do anything about it. And if you think the spill at Valdez was bad, wait till you see a major spill beneath the polar cap. It could take a hundred years to clean up."

"What do the geologists say?" Lyons asked, his eyes still fixed on those bold slashes in red crayon.

"That depends upon which ones you're talking about," Maggie replied. "Most of the guys I know at the agency are definitely concerned. They're not in a position to officially comment one way or another, but they're concerned. The guys that work for the oil companies, on the other hand, don't even want to know about *ivu*. They say it's just an old Eskimo myth."

"And what do you say?" Blancanales asked, his dark eyes also fixed on those angry red slashes.

"I say that no one, and I mean no one, knows more about the ice than the Eskimo."

Finally, from beneath the cot on which she sat, the woman withdrew a drab-green canvas satchel. From the satchel she then pulled out a handful of plastic folders and a heavy notebook embossed with the words North Slope Inc.

"The corporate bylaws," she said, tapping the notebook with her index finger. "Ever since the Native Claims Act, the Eskimo have been running their affairs and managing their land through a natively controlled corporate body. Now, of course, the federal government still retains a natural-resource clause. But if you want to institute some sort of major program, you've ultimately got to face the corporate vote."

"Which means that if the oil companies want to drill offshore, they've got to get the Eskimo vote," Schwarz put in. "Is that basically the story here?"

"Exactly."

"And with sixty billion at stake," Blancanales added, "I assume that the oil companies are not too happy about that."

"Not unless they can stack the deck," Maggie said. "Which is what I think Eddie Frank's murder was all about—stacking the deck in order to make sure that the offshore drilling program is endorsed by the native community."

She rose to her feet, arching a moment to stretch before moving toward the tiny window behind the bunk. Although her face remained taut with fear, it was finally obvious that she was utterly exhausted.

"Now, I don't necessarily believe that the major oil companies are involved in anything truly illegal.

ARCO, Chevron— I don't believe that they'd go as far as murder. But there's a certain public relations firm known as the Prudhoe Bay Information Consortium, and it's headed by a couple of guys named Sweeny and Denton. Supposedly they were hired to help push the offshore drilling scheme through, and frankly I think they're capable of anything—*anything*."

Lyons also rose from the cot, and stepped to the window beside her. "Tell us about the Eskimo," he said softly. "Tell us about that shaman business."

She nodded but initially said nothing. Then, finally sinking back down to the cot, she shook her head and sighed. "It's a very old legend, older than you can possibly imagine."

"And what does it say?" Lyons gently prodded.

"That certain members of the Eskimo tribe were able to commune with the spirits. In their own tongue these spirit talkers were called *anatquk*, and they were generally feared by the whole community. Their power came from what was called the *tunarat*, which meant a personal spirit and might be represented by a whale, a fox or a wolf. The *tunarat* was the spirit that taught the magic songs and the secrets of the ice. It was also the force that sometimes took over the body and filled them with tremendous strength."

"And these shamans," Schwarz asked softly, "they're still around?"

She took another deep breath and shrugged. "With the coming of the white man and Christianity, the practice supposedly died out. The songs were lost and the spirits slipped back under the ice. But every once and a while, there are rumors that the shamans are back... very angry, and very powerful."

Lyons slid down the cot beside the woman and gently placed his hand on her shoulder. "You've got to tell me about what you saw that night with Charlie Hobson," he said.

She took another long, slow breath, then shrugged again. "I don't know what I saw. All I know is that it was horrible, horrible and strong."

"Maybe it was some sort of trained wolf," Blancanales suggested softly. "I mean, there are cases on record of that kind of thing."

Maggie shook her head again. "No, it wasn't a trained wolf. It was a man-wolf, a werewolf, what the natives used to call a skinwalker."

"Skinwalker?" Lyons asked.

"A shaman who puts on the skin of a wolf, and then literally becomes that wolf. For the most part it's associated with the Southwest Indians. The Navaho shamans, for example, are famous for it. But every so often you'll hear of it popping up around here, and then sooner or later somebody always gets killed."

"SO?" BLANCANALES ASKED as he poured another finger of Wild Turkey.

He was seated on a packing crate at the far end of the hut. Maggie Defoe had finally fallen asleep. The grays of evening had darkened to a vaguely incandescent blue. Schwarz, having grown a little restless, had begun to examine an ancient shortwave radio that had once been part of the nation's Early Warning System.

"So nothing," Lyons finally replied from the deeper gloom. "We proceed with a standard investigation. We have a talk with the locals, with the native leaders and with the people out at Prudhoe Bay."

"And that shaman stuff?" Blancanales asked, slipping into the gloom beside Lyons.

"Irrelevant," Lyons replied. "As far as we're concerned, there's just two kinds of forces out there—friendly and unfriendly."

"But what do we do about Maggie?" Blancanales inquired, nodding to her huddled form at the far end of the hut. "I mean, we can't drag her along—she'll just slow us down."

Lyons glanced over his shoulder. In the faint light of the kerosene lamps, the sleeping woman might have been just a girl... alone, afraid and defenseless.

"Until we can get her on a plane and out of the area," he finally said, "I guess Gadgets here will just have to play baby-sitter for a couple of days."

Schwarz looked up from the gutted radio and scratched his head. "Why me?"

"Because if something goes wrong with our communication links, you're the only one who knows how to fix the shortwave." Then, glancing back over his shoulder to Maggie, he grinned. "Besides, you're the only one old enough to be trusted with her."

7

Maggie Defoe was still sleeping when Lyons and Blancanales prepared themselves to face the cold of the sixty-foot walk to the shed where the Cherokee had been parked.

"Anything goes wrong," Lyons told Schwarz as he slipped into his parka, "you get on the radio and call us. Meanwhile, I'll make sure you're contacted if anything comes through on one of the open channels. All that aside, you can always hightail it out on the ATV. Maybe get yourself up to the military base at the point."

Schwarz shifted his gaze east to the seemingly limitless wastes beyond the ice-encrusted chain-link fence. He tried to imagine how it would feel driving for his life in an All Terrain Vehicle, driving through the bone-cracking cold and the solid wall of fog. "Sure. Anything goes wrong, I'll just start up the old ATV," he finally said.

Lingering a few moments longer in the doorway, Blancanales added another last word of advice. "But just in case," he told Schwarz with a smile, "you might want to think about forging yourself a few silver bullets... if you know what I mean."

Although Schwarz managed to return the smile, there was clearly something uneasy about the way he scanned the glowing landscape beyond the chain-link perimeter.

ALTHOUGH MAGGIE HAD HAD the presence of mind to keep the Cherokee plugged in to a battery-operated heater, it still took Blancanales more than twenty minutes to start the engine. It then took another fifteen minutes to clear the frost from the headlights, the windshield and the wipers. There was also frost on the perimeter gates, so that Blancanales finally had to hack off the lock with a hammer.

They moved out slowly, Lyons carefully testing the feel of the road until well past the gates of the facility. The sky was still clear, but another low ice fog was moving in from the north. There were also wisps of fog to the west, where the glacier winds continued to sing.

"So, what's our next move?" Blancanales asked, peering out to the bleak road ahead.

Lyons slowed for a long, gentle turn in the road. "First we get back to Barrow and try to figure out a way to get warm. Then we start asking questions."

"And you think Gadgets and Maggie will be safe out there?"

Lyons hesitated, glancing into the rearview mirror for at least two seconds. "I think they'll be safer than we are," he said.

The Able Team warrior drove in silence for another three or four minutes before he said, "You know something, Pol? I do believe we have a problem behind us."

Although it was still partially obscured by banks of white ice fog, Blancanales also caught a glimpse of something behind them—the hulking gray form of a

Chevy wide-body, with massive snow tires and a customized grill. The driver appeared to be a short, stocky male, possibly a native. The passenger was big, bearded and obviously white. Someone much smaller peered over the dashboard between them.

"Could be fellow travelers," he said. "Another happy party of Arctic motorists on this cold road of life." But just as he made that suggestion, he glimpsed the bearded passenger in the Chevy lift and cock what may have been a short-barreled automatic rifle. "But I seriously don't think so," he said, revising his earlier statement.

"So how do you want to play it?"

Lyons shook his head again. "I'm not sure."

There were large chunks of filthy ice along the seaward edge of the road to Browerville, and Lyons had to slow as he banked into a hard turn. The turn was followed by a relatively long and straight stretch of road between the freshwater lakes. It was the perfect opportunity for the first shattering burst of autofire.

Lyons swerved left across an embankment of moss and into a patch of brittle grass. A second burst sent a spray of glass into the cab of the Cherokee and peppered Blancanales's face with tiny cuts. Lyons caught another glimpse of the passenger's assault rifle and decided that it must be a CAR-15. Then, catching sight of the flashing muzzle, he saw nothing except the blur of brown muskeg grass and white ice.

The Cherokee came to a stop amid blocks of candled ice and a patch of dead grass. After grabbing their deer rifles, Lyons and Blancanales kicked open the doors of the vehicle and slipped down to the ground. A hundred feet away the Chevy now sat by the side of the highway—empty, silent.

"So what do you think?" Blancanales whispered, his face now looking as if he had just shaved while under the influence.

Lyons sank a little deeper into the grass and peered out from the edge of the Cherokee's tire. Between where the Cherokee had come to a stop and the road where the Chevy now sat, lay more than thirty yards of ice-littered field. The ice, in long white blocks, looked like the fallen columns of some ancient ruin. There were also taller blocks here and there, heavy white chunks of ice where any number of figures could be hiding.

"I think we'd better get ourselves a little distance," Lyons said at last. "And I think you'd better zip up your parka."

They moved out on their bellies, keeping to the shadows of the ice blocks. Closer to the sea they heard the calls of the herring gulls. Otherwise, however, it was still dead-quiet.

"Maybe we should try negotiating," Blancanales whispered as they slid into the deeper shadows of an ice block. "Considering there are three of them and that I've only got eight rounds, maybe we should try a little dialogue."

Lyons rose to his knees for a quick glimpse over the ice to the road behind them. He saw the three figures hurry into deeper grass and shook his head. "I don't know, Pol. Something tells me that these guys mean business."

"Yeah, but what about the little one?" Blancanales asked, catching another glimpse of the strange small figure that seemed to hobble between the long columns of ice.

There were patches of dry, granular snow in the shadows of the larger ice blocks, then another clear passage between two more triangular blocks of ice. Lyons entered the clear stretch on his belly, the deer rifle resting in the crook of his arms. Suddenly hearing what must have been the bolt-assist closing mechanism on the CAR-15, he laid the rifle down and withdrew his .45 auto.

A 4-round burst sent clouds of powdered ice high into the air. A long shard of blue ice drew blood on Lyons's knuckles. But having finally caught sight of the hooded rifleman, having actually caught sight of his bearded face, Lyons dropped back down to his belly and fired.

He squeezed off three fast rounds, saw the hooded figure tumble back with the impact of the big slugs and squeezed off another three rounds. Lyons heard the unmistakable groan of bloody pain and then what may have been the ragged breath from a sucking wound.

The Able Team warrior wedged himself a little tighter against the ice block as Blancanales slowly sank a little deeper into the bluish shadows.

"Any idea where the other two are?" Blancanales finally whispered.

"Maybe," Lyons replied softly. "Maybe."

He withdrew a spare magazine from the deepest pocket of his parka, then moved out again on his belly. He was losing the feeling in his left hand. But having finally begun to understand the terrain, to understand the shadows and the ice, Lyons was no longer concerned about the cold. He was no longer really concerned about anything, except ending it.

He continued on his belly until he reached another jagged wedge of ice. Then he rose to his knees again and dropped the safety on his .45 auto. His enemies may have held the early advantage of surprise and firepower, he told himself, but ultimately they had badly underestimated their opponents. They had taken Lyons and Blancanales for a couple of federal flat-feet, and now they were learning the truth.

Lyons hesitated where the candled ice fell away to a long stretch of bare grass. There were cries of more migrating birds, and the wind across smooth sheets of ice sounded almost like a woman sighing. But there was no mistaking the grunt of pain as the wounded rifleman eased himself up over a low wedge of ice and let loose with another burst of autofire.

Lyons squeezed off three rounds as he dropped to his belly again—three quick rounds above the icy columns that littered the field ahead. He heard the heavy slugs from the CAR-15 pound into the ice behind him, then heard another agonized groan as his own slugs hit home. The rifleman rose with the impact, briefly becoming a barrel-chested figure in a gray-green parka before shuddering in a storm of blood and collapsing back down between the long wedges of ice.

It was again very quiet, with only the stiff Arctic breeze and the cries of the frantic birds.

Blancanales appeared, moving almost soundlessly in from between the long rows of candled ice. "That wasn't too hard now, was it?" he said softly, his eyes scanning the scattered ice blocks ahead, the road and the motionless van.

Lyons took a deep breath and then nodded to indicate another massive slab of shore-fast ice. "How about we try for a little elevation?" he whispered.

Pol hefted the deer rifle off his shoulder, and shifted his gaze to the triangular mound of ice. "Looks pretty exposed to me."

"Hey, don't worry." Lyons grinned. "I'll cover you."

Blancanales took a last quick look across the field before moving out. Then, rising to a low crouch, he threaded his way between the frozen debris and into the shadows of that shore-fast mound. Like Lyons, his approach had finally become academic. Although still a little uncomfortable in the frozen terrain, he had definitely slipped into the groove of the kill. He had weighed the odds, analyzed his enemy's methods, and now it was simply a matter of finishing it. There was still something about the third little figure that bothered him, but mainly he focused on simply finishing the hit once and for all.

Blancanales paused at the base of the frozen mound of shore-fast ice. It rose nearly twenty feet above the field and would obviously afford a clear view of the surrounding terrain. But the face of the mound was sheer and exposed, badly exposed.

He hesitated another twenty or thirty seconds, peering out across the ice-littered field. Dropping the safety on the deer rifle, he rose and began to climb. He moved slowly at first, testing the ridges and the wind-sheered face. He paused again at ten feet, pressing himself into the ice and scanning the field again. Then, gradually dragging himself to the top, he finally caught sight of his enemy.

It took about four seconds for Blancanales to bring the deer rifle up to his shoulder, aim and fire—four hard seconds. Sixty feet across the field, a dark figure rose from behind a wedge of ice, wielding another

CAR-15. Blancanales saw the man's face, the distinctive Eskimo features screwed into an intense moment of concentration. He saw the man's eyes narrow with hatred and the lips draw back to reveal his teeth. He also saw the stubby barrel of the fully-automatic CAR rifle, and he knew he couldn't wait any longer.

He squeezed off two shots in the face of the automatic spray, two clean shots that lifted the Eskimo off his feet and tossed him back over the columns of ice. Then, watching the stricken man rise again and bring the CAR around for a last desperate burst, Blancanales squeezed off a third shot that literally blew the man away and left him among the brittle Arctic grass.

A number of things went through Blancanales's mind as he pressed himself back down to the mound of ice and began to scan the field in search of the third figure he'd seen in the Chevy. He recalled the fleeting vision of the little man hobbling across the barren field and wondered why a pair of obviously seasoned killers would have brought such a strange creature along for the ride. He also acknowledged that although his training and experience had served him well thus far, there was still probably a great deal that he did not understand about this land and about these people. Finally, he supposed, there was undoubtedly much he had to learn about what may have lived out here, about the bears, the foxes and the wolves.

He was still scanning the horizon, still thinking about how much he did not know about this world, when he heard the low snarl of a creature behind him. But with speed gained only from his experiences during previous missions, he rolled on his back because that was the fastest way to bring the deer rifle around.

It was then that he saw the gray blur of fur and the flash of white teeth.

The creature seemed to drop from nowhere, as if it had suddenly materialized out of thin air. It came hard and fast, and there was something ghostly about its eyes, which were definitely human eyes set deep inside the head of a wolf.

Blancanales spun again, tucking his head under his left arm, bringing up the rifle with his right. But the creature's fury and its strength were unbelievable. Blancanales kicked out blindly as its teeth tore into his parka, peeling away four inches of reinforced lining. He heard the sound of ripping nylon, felt the fetid breath on his face and the pressure of the paws on his chest. He heard himself screaming in stark terror, while a calmer and more rational part of him told him to cover his throat.

Then he heard the shots from below, three rapid bursts from Lyons's auto that left the creature momentarily stiff and shuddering, until it finally leaped off the ice with a howling scream.

Blancanales caught one more glimpse of the thing before it vanished into the fog. For a moment, no more than a fraction of a second, he thought he saw the wolf's head fall away and a human head emerge. But given the fog and the distance, he really couldn't be sure.

He turned and watched Lyons approach slowly, his .45 still dangling from his right hand, the deer rifle casually resting on his shoulder. Although Pol was fairly certain he hadn't been seriously hurt, he couldn't seem to stand, couldn't seem to move his damn leg. Then, finally taking a deep breath and shaking it off, he slowly began to slide back down the ice mound.

"You all right?" Lyons asked as he drew closer. "Hey, Pol, you all right?" he repeated when Blancanales failed to respond.

Blancanales was gently examining the shredded parka and the flakes of bloody flesh on his shoulder. "Yeah," he said at last. "I'm all right."

From where they stood, both bodies were visible. There was the bearded white man who Lyons had nailed with his .45 and the stocky Eskimo who Blancanales had tagged with the deer rifle. Apart from a few smeared prints and a thin trail of blood, however, there were no traces of the werewolf.

Blancanales turned back to the mound and knelt on the ice to examine the prints—man-sized, but definitely not human.

"If I were you," Lyons said, "I wouldn't even think about it. You know what I'm saying? You start trying to figure it out based on what you saw, and it's going to drive you crazy. So I wouldn't even waste my time thinking about it right now."

Blancanales placed a gloved hand on the print, then traced the outline of the animal's pads with his index finger. "All right, then you tell me. What was it? Hmm? What the hell was that thing?"

Lyons shrugged. "I don't know. Maybe it was a trained dog or something."

"One that walks on two legs? Come on, Carl, how the hell are you going to train a dog to walk on two legs? How are you going to train a dog to attack like that on only two legs?"

"All right, so maybe it was a little guy in some kind of wolf suit."

"Then how did he move like that, huh? How did he move so damn fast?"

Blancanales turned to face the half-frozen sea and the glow of light off the ice sheets. "And I'll tell you something else about that thing," he said softly. "I may not have gotten a good look at it, but I smelled it. I smelled it real good, and it definitely did not smell like a man. It smelled like a wolf."

8

There was a lot that the constable and his deputy did not want to know. The constable was a short, round Eskimo named Will Tipper. His deputy was a thin, mustached boy from Oregon named Woody. They were the remaining authority figures in the North Slope Borough and they resented the workload that seemed to be headed their way.

"So you say those two guys attacked you, huh?" Tipper asked in his slow, native drawl. He was gazing out across the rows of candled ice to the bodies.

"That's right," Lyons said. "They attacked us."

"From that Chevy, you say?"

"That's right, from the Chevy."

"Then they drove you off the road and into that field?" Tipper asked.

"That's right."

"And that's where you shot 'em?"

"Yeah, that's where we shot them—in self-defense."

After a moment or two of dull silence, Tipper simply shrugged. "Well, that makes sense."

Although the sun had finally dropped below the white horizon, the sky continued to glow. It was also strangely warmer and the wind had died to a mere whisper.

Tipper stepped down from his hardtop Jeep Eagle, and slowly tramped forward across the icy field. His deputy followed with a clipboard under one arm, a shotgun under the other. When the Jeep had first appeared, rolling out of the fog from Barrow, Blancanales and Lyons had stepped out of the Cherokee and cocked their weapons...just in case. After taking one look at the motley pair, however, they had simply shrugged and stepped back into the comparative warmth.

"Any idea who they are?" Lyons asked, stepping up behind Tipper and the deputy.

Tipper bent from the waist, Eskimo-style, to examine the now blue-gray face of the bearded corpse between the blocks of bloody ice. "Nope," he finally breathed. "Never seen him before."

"What about the other one?" Blancanales asked, indicating the body of the native sprawled forty feet away.

Tipper turned, tramping between two more long columns of shattered ice. "Nope, don't know him, either," he claimed as he examined the native's face.

"Which means what?" Lyons asked. "That they're not from here?"

Tripper nodded. "That's right. They're not from around here."

Next, Tipper examined the fully automatic CAR-15s. He pried the first one out of the bearded man's hands, worked the slide a couple of times and then handed the piece to his deputy.

"So?" Blancanales asked.

Tipper shrugged. "So, not too many people around here use that kind of thing. In fact, nobody around here uses that type of weapon."

"So where do you think they came from?" Lyons asked.

But Tipper merely shrugged again. "Who knows?"

The constable's "investigation," concluded with a cursory inspection of the abandoned Chevy. Apart from three empty whiskey bottles, a stack of *Playboys*, and a mess of peanut shells, however, there was nothing—no registration, no license plates, nothing.

"I think you'll probably find that it was stolen," Lyons said.

Tipper continued to peer in through the open door, then shifted his gaze to the ground around the vehicle. "Yeah," he finally sighed. "It was probably stolen."

"You still might want to check for prints, however," Lyons added.

"Sure," Tipper nodded. "We could check for prints, except that no one around here knows anything about prints." He turned suddenly to face Lyons with a strangely probing glance. "But we do know a thing or two about tracks."

Lyons held the lawman's gaze for three or four seconds before finally cocking his head with a thin smile. "Okay, what's your point?"

Tipper slowly stepped around to the side of the Chevy and nodded to the ground at his feet. "Three sets of footprints," he said. "You told me that two guys tried to shoot you, and you showed me two bodies. So how come I see three sets of footprints here?"

Lyons dropped his gaze to the boot tracks in the icy mud and snow, and nodded. "Good question."

The on-site investigation ended on a patch of ground beside the constable's Jeep. The deputy had produced a flask of brandy from his parka, but only

Blancanales was interested. Tipper had radioed the medical center and then began to pencil in a homicide report. Lyons rested on the still-warm hood of the Jeep, gazing out to the white wastes.

"I guess I don't have to tell you boys to stick around town for a while, do I?" Tipper said, pausing to lick the tip of his pencil.

"No," Lyons said. "You don't have to tell us to stick around."

"I also guess I don't have to tell you that I may be wanting to talk to your superiors in Washington—or wherever your superiors are."

"That could probably be arranged," Lyons replied, "if necessary."

"And finally I shouldn't have to tell you that this business may not exactly be over just yet."

"No," Lyons answered. "You don't have to tell me that, either."

"And just because you boys got lucky here today, it don't mean you're going to be lucky the next time. Because this here is Eskimo land, and white people don't always have much luck out here, especially when they're up against a skinwalker."

Lyons turned and looked at the man. "A skinwalker, Constable?"

Tipper nodded to the strange set of footprints leading from the abandoned Chevy and vanishing out on the ice. "Oh, I think you know what I'm talking about, Mr. Lyons. I think you know exactly what I'm talking about."

IT WAS WELL INTO the evening when Lyons and Blancanales finally returned to their room at the Sheffield Hotel.

"Listen to this," Blancanales said. He was seated on the edge of the bed with a paperback book he had picked up from a dusty rack in the lobby. The book was entitled *Arctic Folk and Fancy*, and there was a photograph of a rampant polar bear on the cover. "It says here that there was once a shaman from Barrow, whose spirit was a gray wolf. Whenever the shaman put on a wolf's skin and began to dance, his feet became the feet of a wolf, and his teeth—"

"Why don't you give it a rest, Pol?" Lyons interrupted. He was still poised at the window, still gazing down the darkened streets.

"I'm just trying to—"

"I know what you're trying to do, and there's no mileage in it. You understand what I'm saying? There's just no mileage in it."

"All right, then you tell me. You tell me what the hell attacked me out there. Huh? You tell me what the hell that thing was."

Lyons shrugged. "Like I said before, it could have been a lot of things. It happened so fast that it could have been a—a trained dog, some guy in a wolf's suit, a lot of things."

"And what if wasn't one of those things? What if it was something that..." He broke off and shook his head with a hard sigh. "Hey, I'm sorry. I think this place is just starting to get to me. You know what I mean?"

Lyons nodded, his eyes still fixed on the frozen desolation beyond the rooftops. "Yeah," he said. "I know exactly what you mean."

9

Little by little the icy desolation had begun to wear on Gadgets Schwarz. Twice he found himself instinctively reaching for his weapon at the sound of the wind through loose sheets of metal. He had also found himself continually returning to the tiny frosted square of Plexiglas, where he gazed anxiously into the twilight.

It was just after midnight. Although the horizon continued to glow with gray-blue light, the Quonset hut was now bathed in shadows. Maggie Defoe remained hunched at her battered desk, poring over maps of the Slope and plotting the floe with a pocket calculator. Now and again she had found herself jumping at the echo of the wind through the rafters and the rattle of loose sheet-metal. But mostly it was her calculations that frightened her—her mathematical projection of what would happen if an offshore rig began pouring crude oil under the ice.

"Know anything about the ice?" she asked after a long spell of silence.

Schwarz turned from the window and shook his head. "Not really."

"Well, the pack is kind of a like a gyre. It spins in a slow clockwise circle around the Beaufort Sea. You get a major *ivu* crush on an offshore drill, and you could end up with a spill beneath the ice that would never disperse. There would be no black ice, no floating animals, but one day the wildlife would simply be gone . . . forever."

Schwarz stepped away from the window and sank to one of the narrow cots. "So what's your point?" he finally asked.

She leaned back in her chair and ran her fingers through her tawny mane of hair. "My point is," she said softly, "this isn't just about Eddie Frank's death. It's not even about Charlie Hobson's death. It's about the future of the whole Arctic Circle. If the oil companies start drilling offshore, they could end up pouring crude under the ice. And if that happens, the entire ecosystem could crash—the whales, the seals, the fish, the bears, the wolves . . . all dead."

"And you think that's why Frank was killed? Because he knew about it?"

"All the old Eskimo know about it," she said. "They can't necessarily prove it scientifically, but they know it."

As Schwarz got up to return to the window, the Able Team warrior was suddenly aware that either the wind had shifted or someone was attempting to cut through the compound gates. He was also fairly certain that he heard the drone of an idling engine.

"Did you hear that?" Maggie whispered, her eyes suddenly wide with fear.

"Yeah," he said calmly, actually glad at the prospect of a confrontation. "I heard it."

"It could just be a bear," she added hopefully. "There are a lot of bears around here."

"Yeah. Maybe it's just a bear."

But by this time he had already withdrawn his .45 auto and cocked it.

Gadgets moved to the bureau and extinguished two of the three kerosene lanterns. He heard another strange noise, but he ignored it and continued working in the half light. He decided that, as a first line of defense, he had to rearrange the furniture. He had to construct a firing post with the bureaus, filing cabinets and heaps of damp newspapers. He had to lay a trip wire across the doorway. As an added obstacle to anyone attempting to break through the door, he poured a pint of kerosene across the linoleum.

After hastily completing this first line of defense, he picked up the deer rifle and crouched down beside Maggie. The immediate vicinity was still quiet.

"You know how to use one of these?" he asked, easing a cartridge into the chamber.

She tentatively extended a hand and ran her fingertips along the smooth grain of the stock. "I think so," she whispered.

"All right, then I want you to stay down and shoot anything that comes in that door."

"What about you?"

He picked up a flashlight, slipped it into the pocket of his parka and then zipped up. "I'm going to go take a look outside."

IT WAS COLDER than he had imagined and the glow along the horizon only vaguely lighted the landscape. Maybe it *was* a bear, he told himself as he scanned the empty compound. Maybe it was just some old polar bear looking for a little dinner. Then, from the adjacent shed that had once served as the radio room, he definitely heard the sound of metal against metal.

He dropped the safety on his .45 and slipped into the shadows of the radio tower. Beyond the tower lay an open stretch of mossy gravel, then the hut that had probably once housed the enlisted men, then the hut where Maggie had left the All Terrain Vehicle. Although his view of the last two shacks was still obscured by the darkness, he was almost certain that the doors were now ajar.

He moved out again in a low crouch, keeping to the balls of his feet. Although the breeze was like a razor blade across his face, his back was now wet with perspiration and his gloved hand was moist around the butt of his weapon. But when he finally reached the doorway of the radio shack, he couldn't have felt calmer.

He hesitated beside the open door of the radio room to listen. Hearing nothing above the wind through the overhead wires, he dropped down to another crouch and withdrew the flashlight from his parka.

There were all sorts of theories concerning how one best entered a potentially dangerous room. Talk to a cop, and he'll tell you that your best friend is surprise—a hard and fast rush that catches the occupants completely unaware. Talk to a cat burglar, and he'll tell you to take it slow—slow and easy like a panther moving through a jungle. To Schwarz's mind, however, the key was not in the speed of the entrance, but in the method. The average gunman was right-handed and untrained. That meant he tended to shoot high and to the left. Therefore, when entering a room, you wanted to stay low and to the right....

Schwarz took his own advice, moving low and to the left, keeping his gun arm stiff and extended while his left hand trained the flashlight to the far wall.

He waited a full three seconds before rising, three taut seconds while he swept the flashlight across the walls. Then, finally realizing that he was all alone, he rose to inspect the damage.

The shortwave equipment had been stacked on a low steel table against the far wall. At first glance Schwarz concluded that the sabotage had been hasty and by no means complete. Upon closer inspection, however, he saw that the saboteur had known exactly what he was doing—the cables were cut, the components smashed and the transistors had been removed.

From the radio shack he moved quickly to the storage shed where the All Terrain Vehicle had been stored. There, too, the sabotage had been complete—tires slashed, distributor cap gone, fan and drive belts cut. For what seemed like a long time, he simply stood in the shadow of the compound gates and scanned the landscape around him.

"WHAT DO WE DO NOW?" Maggie asked once Schwarz had explained the situation to her. She was still crouched behind the wall of filing cabinets, still clutching the deer rifle.

"We wait," Schwarz replied.

"But your friends will be back, right? I mean when they don't hear from us, they'll be back."

"Sure," Schwarz breathed. "When they don't hear from us, they'll be back."

"Then we really don't have anything to worry about, right? *Right?*"

Schwarz moved to the frosted square of Plexiglas adjacent to the door. Although the wind had faded to a gentle breeze, there was definitely something moving in on the horizon—fog, snow, something. "That's right," he finally sighed. "We don't have anything to worry about."

10

"Maybe we should give Gadgets a call," Blancanales suggested.

It was dawn, or what passed for dawn in the Arctic. Although neither man had slept more than three or four hours, the time for sleep was over.

"So how about it?" Blancanales persisted. "You want me to go down to the lobby and give Gadgets a honk on the shortwave?"

Lyons stepped back from the window, dragging his thermal sweatshirt over his muscled torso. "Unnecessary risk," he said at last. "As far as anyone knows, Gadgets and Maggie could be anywhere—east, west, anywhere. I really don't see the point in risking a triangulation of their radio signal for a good-morning call. Besides, if they need us, they'll call."

"Then how about we get something to eat?" Blancanales said, also shedding his thermal undershirt.

Lyons glanced at his field watch, then back out to the street and the frozen shore beyond. "How about we grab a piece of whale blubber and eat on the run. There's some questions I want to ask, and I'm tired of waiting for the answers."

THE MOST OBVIOUS indication of the presence of oil money in Barrow was the offices of the North Slope

Borough. A large, blue-roofed building delivered in pieces from the south, it was the tallest structure in the community. Inside, there were long corridors laid with plush red carpet, polychromed prints of whalers among the icebergs and a closed-circuit television system. Although most of the offices were empty, there were still the smells of habitation: caribou steak, after-shave and marijuana.

The receptionist was a pretty native woman with long, braided hair and too much eyeliner. The mayor, she told Lyons and Blancanales, was in Fairbanks attending the annual All Native Conference. But if Lyons and Blancanales so desired, she could probably arrange a meeting with the mayor's assistant and vice president of the Arctic Slope Regional Corporation.

"Does he know what's going on around here?" Lyons asked.

The woman replied with a sleepy shrug. "Sure. Mr. Laplin knows what's going on."

Twenty minutes later Lyons and Blancanales found themselves in an office filled with modular chrome-and-glass furniture. Leatherbound law books dominated the far wall, while shelves of native handicrafts framed the window. Behind the polished oak desk sat a bulky Eskimo in banker's gray. Half-submerged in a rich leather chair, he looked a little like a fat toad on a throne. The desk was bare except for a copy of the *Wall Street Journal*, a pen-and-pencil set and a brass paperweight in the shape of an oil derrick.

"Mr. Laplin?" Lyons asked.

The Eskimo nodded, then glanced at Blancanales. "I thought there were supposed to be three of you," he said. "Three big-city enforcement guys, come to teach us Eskimo a thing or two about keeping the peace."

Lyons looked at the man, studying the diamond on his finger and the gold on his watch, trying to figure out how a native could grow so divorced from his roots. "Right now there's just the two of us," he finally said.

Laplin held Lyons's gaze for at least fifteen seconds. Finally settling back into his seat with a smile, he said, "All right, why don't you boys take a seat and tell me what I can do for you?"

The chairs were also leather and obviously expensive. The coffee that the receptionist eventually brought, however, was freeze-dried and too strong.

"It's about what happened to Eddie Frank," Lyons said at last.

Laplin nodded gravely. "Yes, poor Eddie."

"It's also about what happened to Charlie Hobson," Blancanales added.

Laplin picked up the gold pencil from his desk and began to turn it over in his fingers. In addition to his razor-cut hair and the scent of after-shave, he apparently had his nails varnished.

"You know, despite these trappings," he said after a pause, "this is still a very primitive place in many respects. Take a stroll out onto the ice, and suddenly you are no longer in the twentieth century. Suddenly you are in a place that has hardly changed in ten thousand years. There are many dangers out there—the cold, the wind, the bears...all sorts of dangers waiting to claim a man's life. Why, just last year—"

"Somehow I don't think what happened to Eddie Frank and Charlie Hobson had anything to do with natural dangers," Lyons interrupted.

"No?" Laplin asked. "Then what do you think caused their demise?"

Lyons reached across the desk and picked up the tiny brass model of the oil derrick. "This," he said. "This is what I think caused their death."

Laplin placed his fingertips together in a meditative gesture and briefly lowered his gaze in thought. "Let me tell you a little something about the Eskimo," he said at last. "Let me tell you something about oil and the Eskimo."

He then rose from his desk, stepped to the window and drew back the curtains to reveal another slightly terrifying view of the icy wasteland beyond the shore.

"Do you see that?" he said. "For fifteen thousand years that was our homeland. That was our world and our universe. It was not a kind place or a bountiful place, but at least it was ours. Then one day the white man came and took it away from us. Not all at once, of course, but little by little he took it away. Finally, in 1971, the white man took pity on us and gave us some of the land back in what they called the Native Claims Settlement Act. Not that what we received was really a gift. Oh, no, we had to fight for it. We had to fight tooth and claw for every damn acre. But when it was over, we had some of our land back, and we had a real live profit-making corporation to administer that land—the Arctic Slope Regional Corporation."

Laplin turned from the window and moved to a framed map of the Arctic hung on the adjacent wall. "Now, you see this?" he asked. "This is our land today. This is what we have achieved through political struggle—the North Slope Borough, the largest native-owned and native-controlled administrative body in the world. Depending upon how you choose to count, there are thirteen regional corporations, with forty million acres to administer. This is what the white man's Congress gave us. Forty million acres of ice. And what do you suppose we can do with these acres, hmm? Hunt on them? Fish on them? No, these acres are not for hunting and fishing, not really. These acres are for taxing the white men who have finally discovered oil on Eskimo land."

Laplin returned to his desk and sank back into his red leather chair. "A lot of white people come up here, you know, and they say how terrible it is that the Eskimo has lost his traditional way of life. They say how terrible it is that the Congress set up profit-making corporations to turn the Eskimo people into capitalists. They say how terrible it is that little Eskimo children are now taught how to buy and sell stock and how to invest the money earned from their shares of the corporation. They also say how terrible it is that the Eskimo no longer relies on the elders for counsel, but instead relies on big-city lawyers and big-city accountants. Terrible, they say. Tragic. Well, let me tell you something. Eskimo never had it so good, not in over five thousand years."

Lyons shifted his gaze to the map on the wall: red pins to indicate the regional corporations, blue pins to indicate the governmental offices and green pins to indicate the oil fields. "We're not here to judge your life-styles," he said at last. "We're just here to find out what happened to Eddie Frank and Charlie Hobson."

"And what if I were to tell you that Eddie and Charlie died on the ice, and that's all anyone needs to know?" Laplin said gravely.

"Then I'd have to tell you that it's not enough," Lyons replied.

Blancanales spoke next, his eyes leveled directly at Laplin, his voice flat and cold. "See, we're real sticklers for details," he said. "We heard that two men died on the ice, and we can't seem to keep ourselves from wondering about the details."

Laplin smiled, shaking his head slightly. "You want details? Okay, I'll give you details. You know how much money Eskimo are going to make from this oil? How about close to a billion dollars. Now, that's a detail for you. That's a real detail."

Lyons rose from his chair and moved to the chrome-and-glass shelves along the far wall. Among the native artifacts on display were two tiny wolves cut from walrus ivory: one sleeping, the other hunched in rage.

"You know what they've been saying about Frank and Hobson?" he asked casually. "They've been saying that a shaman killed them, a shaman in the shape of a wolf."

Laplin smiled again, with another slight shake of his head. "That's the trouble with Eskimo," he said. "Even though they're now big corporate stockholders, they still can't shake off the old superstitions. They still can't keep themselves from singing to the whales and tossing the bones in order to tell the future."

"They also say that the wolf still walks the ice," Lyons added. "They say that he still walks the ice in search of people who ask too many questions about the oil companies."

Laplin started to smile again, but the smile suddenly froze in a kind of feral grimace. There was also something hard and feral in his coal-black eyes and the furrowed brow. "That's a very dangerous accusation, Mr. Lyons, very dangerous indeed."

"It also may be the truth, Mr. Laplin."

"Then in that case I suggest that you, too, stay off the ice, Mr. Lyons, because an Arctic wolf is just as likely to go for a white man's throat as an Eskimo's throat..."

IT WAS NOON when Lyons and Blancanales left the headquarters of the North Slope Borough...another dull noon, with ice fog moving in from the bay and a breeze that smelled of ancient glaciers. All along the streets of Barrow, native teenagers in sunglasses continued to slouch in the doorways or against the hoods of their Chevys and Fords. There were also a number of sleeping drunks here and there, and the pungent stench of dog shit.

"So what's next?" Blancanales asked, pausing to watch a line of native women in front of the general store. Farther along the street, amid scrap lumber and the gutted shell of a Honda Civic, lay two or three caribou heads and the carcass of a seal.

Lyons let his gaze rest on the heap of garbage, then finally took a deep breath. "We keep asking people questions," he said at last.

"Any people in particular?"

Lyons shifted his gaze to a black limousine parked in the shadows along a side street—the outline of a gold oil derrick was stenciled on the gleaming door. Although the windows were smoked, it was fairly obvious that the occupants were meeting Lyons's gaze full on.

"Might as well start with those people right there," Lyons said as two angular men in cowboy hats emerged from the limousine, the suggestive bulge of weapons obvious beneath their trench coats.

11

The two men approached slowly, their hands in the pockets of their coats. The taller one was thin and lanky, with steel-gray hair and what might have been a razor scar along his jaw. The shorter one was built like a fighter. As they drew closer, the taller man forced a tight smile and introduced himself as Jim. The other one wanted to be called Larry. The limousine, Jim said, had been specially requested, and drinks were on the house.

Lyons shifted his gaze from the lanky one to the short one, and then back again. "So basically you want us to take a little ride with you—is that what's going on here?"

Jim nodded, his lips stretching into another tight smile. "That's right, sir. We would be much obliged if you and your associate would join us."

"And where exactly are we going?" Blancanales wondered.

Jim cocked his head to the south. "Airstrip."

"And then?" Lyons asked.

Jim cocked his head to the east. "Prudhoe Bay."

Several things went through Lyons's mind as he quickly exchanged a glance with Blancanales and then leveled his gaze on the strangers again. He mentally calculated the distance between his right foot and the taller man groin, but then decided that the safest and most effective opening move would be a skipping side-thrust to the knee. He noted that the shorter man still had his right hand concealed in his pocket, and wondered what sort of weapon was hidden there and how fast it would come into play. Not fast enough, he decided, if Blancanales also opened with a skipping kick. But at the same time, he thought about what could be learned from the oilmen at Prudhoe Bay and how it was always advantageous to walk in with an invitation.

"All right, boys. Let's take a ride," he finally said.

TWO HUNDRED MILES STRETCHED between the Eskimo community at Barrow and the oil fields at Prudhoe Bay—two hundred miles and two thousand years. From the air and in the thin light of a spring afternoon, the installation at Prudhoe Bay looks like a lunar station, with a geometric assemblage of prefabricated dormitories and long lines of silver pipes.

It was cold and clear when the little six-seater touched down on the strip. Although Lyons and Blancanales had been repeatedly offered single-malt Scotch, they had only accepted orange juice. En route Jim had mainly discussed the food at Prudhoe Bay. "We serve our boys the same kind of steaks they used to serve the Rangers in Nam," he said. "We also got Canadian lobster," he added, "and the best damn burgers you ever tasted."

A second limousine was waiting at the strip. The driver was an Oriental and he welcomed the Able Team commandos to Prudhoe Bay.

Closer to the main complex lay more ranks of gleaming storage tanks, a network of pipes and a row of prefabricated dormitories on stilts above the tundra. Then came the fences, what looked like armed guard towers and finally the consortium's headquarters.

A long, paved walk led from the road to the entrance of the executive offices. There were cameras on the surrounding towers and uniformed guards wearing sunglasses. The doors were steel and apparently bullet proof. Hidden speakers played country-western ballads. The floors were covered with burgundy carpets and the walls were paneled with varnished pine.

"Well, this here is as far as I go," Jim said as they entered the lobby. "But don't you worry none, because your enjoyment has been assured. And I do mean *assured*." Tipping his ten-gallon hat, he moved off with Larry into the red plush gloom.

"WELCOME TO the twenty-first century," a slender man in a pin-striped suit greeted Lyons and Blancanales.

His name was Sweeny, he added, although everyone called him "Happy." He was accompanied by a man wearing slacks and a sports jacket who called himself Denton. There was also a pretty blonde named Gracie who brought coffee and croissants.

The office was spacious and vaguely reminiscent of a Texas hunting lodge. There was a fake fireplace with a smoldering plastic log, and the furniture was covered with artificially aged leather. Indian blankets were hung on the wall and an ornate saddle chair filled one corner. There was also an array of high-tech video equipment, a mechanical bar and pool table.

But what ultimately held Lyons's gaze, held it like a magnet for at least thirty seconds, was the stuffed head of an old gray wolf.

"A beauty, ain't it?" Sweeny said from behind the tooled desk.

"Yeah," Lyons growled recalling the vision of that old gray dying on the spine of a hill. "A real beauty."

"Well, now," Sweeny began with a jovial clap of his hands. "I reckon you boys are probably wondering exactly who we are and why we asked you all out here."

"Course they're wondering," Denton put in. "Wouldn't you be?"

But after exchanging another glance with Blancanales, Lyons said only, "Actually I think we pretty much got it all figured out."

At which point, Sweeny sank down to the sofa and nodded. "Well, in that case," he said, "I guess there's really no point in beating around the bush."

Another map of the Arctic appeared—this time mechanically lowered from the ceiling. Among the more obvious points of interest were the projected offshore sites east of Barrow.

"First thing I want to say," Sweeny drawled, "is that we're not actually representing any *one* oil company. No, sir. We are the Prudhoe Bay Information Consortium and we're what you might call an *independent* public relations unit. In other words, we're kind of like a hired hand working in conjunction with all the firms in this here wilderness."

"Independent and autonomous," Denton added. "We've got our own investors and our own charter."

"The next thing I want to say," Sweeny continued, "is that I have no intention of insulting your intelligence by pretending that you boys don't know what issues are at stake here. No, sir, I ain't going to pretend that. Instead, I'm going to say straight out that we asked you here because we want to clear the air of some unpleasant rumors that seem to have been floating around lately."

"Very unpleasant rumors," Denton added.

"For example," Sweeny continued, "we heard that you boys were sent out here as an investigative body to look into the unfortunate demise of a poor Eskimo fellow."

"Two Eskimo," Blancanales said. "There have been two mangled Eskimo so far."

"All right, two Eskimo," Sweeny conceded. "But the fact is, our clients had nothing to do with it."

"And what makes you think that we suspect otherwise?" Lyons asked.

"Oh, come on, Mr. Lyons," Sweeny drawled. "You think I just fell off the applecart, or what? I know that if you boys were sent in all the way from—well, wherever the heck you came from—somebody obviously suspects that those Eskimo deaths are connected to one hell of a major issue. And when you're talking about the North Slope, there's only one major issue—oil."

"Which naturally concerns us," Denton added, "from a public relations standpoint if nothing else."

"So, we just want to clear the air on that subject once and for all," Sweeny continued. "Sure, we may have had a few problems with certain native factions over the years, but we sure as hell don't play dirty with those people. In fact, if you boys weren't who you are, I wouldn't even deem it necessary to make these statements. I mean, after all, we're talking about the outfit that brings this great nation warmth and light. We're talking about the company that supplies our country with the substance of life. We're talking about oil!"

There was a slightly awkward silence following this speech, and for a long time Lyons and Blancanales simply stared at their hosts.

Finally, cocking his head, Denton added softly, "I think what Happy here is trying to say is that we are not the enemy. We are not attempting to destroy the Eskimo way of life or their environment. All we're attempting to do is to provide this nation with the means to grow, the means to fuel an economy without a dependence on foreign sources. Now, I realize that at the moment oil and coal shortages may not seem to be the most pressing issue in the world. I mean, you've got your crime problems, your drug problems and your terrorist problems. But unless this nation continues to explore and develop fuel sources, those problems might one day seem minor compared to the energy problem."

"And as for the environment," Sweeny began in an equally soft and sincere voice, "all I can say is that we at the Bay love this nation's natural splendor as much as anyone. But when people start freezing in the dark because some A-rab decided to put the squeeze on us, they're not going to give a damn about a few polar bears and a few seals. All they're going to care about is oil and that's the bottom line."

There was another slightly awkward silence as Lyons and Blancanales continued to wait, with eyes fixed on the hosts, faces virtually expressionless, untouched cups of coffee growing cold on the table in front them.

"Anything else you want to tell us?" Lyons eventually asked, his eyes still showing no expression, his voice still flat and cold.

Another three or four cold seconds passed. Shaking his head, Sweeny said, "No, I think that about does it."

"But we would be awfully obliged if you gentlemen would join us for an afternoon of festivities before we take you home," Denton said.

Beyond the main conference room lay a truly lavish suite that was popularly known as "The Soft Touch Room." The lighting was soft and filtered through tiffany shades. There were daybeds covered in blue silk damask and a low divan upholstered in crushed velvet. Above the fake fireplace hung a lavish portrait of a kneeling courtesan.

"So what do you make of it?" Blancanales whispered, his gaze resting on that strangely enticing portrait of the naked girl.

"I think we'd better get the hell out of here," Lyons said in an equally soft voice.

Explaining that they had a few phone calls to make, Sweeny and Denton had left their guests alone, with whiskey and cognac on a side table, champagne in a bucket of crushed ice, selections of classical music wafting through concealed speakers.

"I also think we'd better assume that the walls have ears," Lyons added softly. Nodding to a gilded mirror in an oval frame, he continued, "And eyes."

Blancanales was still gazing at the portrait of the woman when someone softly knocked at the door. Lyons responded first, stepping to the shelves and quickly looking for some sort of weapon. He finally picked an ivory dagger, probably some sort of native artifact. But before the Able Team warrior had a chance to hide behind the door, it opened.

Two girls entered slowly. The first one was slender and dark, with black hair and vaguely Hispanic features. The second was tall and blond, with very blue eyes. The dark one wore a white, strapless dress and red heels, while the blonde wore a silk evening gown but no shoes.

"I'm Carrie," the blonde said as she slid through the door and fixed her eyes on Lyons.

"And I'm Coco," the other girl announced.

"And I should have known," Lyons said under his breath.

The blonde retrieved four glasses from the cabinet, while Coco began to work the cork from the bottle of champagne.

"I guess you might say we're the welcoming committee," Coco cooed.

"Or the entertainment committee," Carrie added.

Lyons glanced at the oval mirror, wondering just how many eyes were watching. "Yeah? So what's the deal?"

The blonde threw her head back and approached Lyons. "The deal is anything you want," she said softly. Then, sliding her hands around his neck, her lips only inches away from his, she added, "Anything at all."

Coco had finally succeeded in releasing the cork. Filling the glasses with an exaggerated flourish, she moved toward Blancanales. "We just want to have a little party," she said softly. "You know what I mean? A little party?"

Blancanales gently removed her hand from his thigh. "It's not that I don't appreciate the gesture," he said. "It's just that I'm not in the mood right now."

She returned her left hand to his thigh, her right hand to his shoulder. "Well, maybe we can put you in the mood," she whispered.

But when Coco lifted her eyes to Blancanales, she saw nothing even approaching desire. "Well, that's too bad," she sighed. "Let's not waste our time here," she said, turning to Carrie.

The girls left as quickly as they had arrived, leaving Lyons and Blancanales alone in the room once again. From somewhere beyond the walls came the soft hum of generators and what may have been an electric blender. Then they heard voices, followed by footsteps and finally the double click of a cocking automatic.

"Move," Lyons whispered.

Blancanales rose from the corner of the low divan and stepped to the fake fireplace. There he found two reasonably lethal weapons: a twenty-one-inch brass poker and an iron-handled brush. After weighing each in his hand, he finally settled on the poker.

Lyons stepped to the opposite corner of the room and picked up the ivory dagger once again. He tested the point on the palm of his hand, slipped it between his teeth and pressed himself against the wall beside the door. He did not have to wait long. The sound of the turning doorknob immediately put both men on combat alert. Blancanales shifted his eyes to the door; he held the poker loosely in his right hand, partially concealing it behind his back. Although seemingly relaxed, his knees were bent and his muscles were taut.

When the door finally opened, Blancanales relaxed somewhat as he recognized Jim and Larry.

"Hey, what's happening?" Jim grinned from the doorway.

Blancanales cocked his head with an equally broad smile. "Not much."

"Then how about coming for a little ride with us?" Jim drawled.

"Where to?"

The lanky cowboy nodded to his left. "Outside."

"I don't think so," Blancanales said. "I kind of like it right here."

Jim frowned, exchanging a quick glance with Larry. Withdrawing a long-barreled .22 automatic from his blazer, he said, "Well, that's a shame. That's really a shame, because I sure as hell didn't want to ruin this here pretty carpet with your guts."

Larry had also withdrawn his weapon, but despite the display of firepower, Jim suddenly grew concerned, wary.

"Say, Blanc," he said softly. "Where's your buddy?"

"My buddy?" Blancanales asked, his right hand growing marginally tighter around the poker.

"That Lyons fellow. Where's Lyons?" Without waiting for a reply, he took another step forward.

Two full seconds passed before Lyons made his move. Jim had finally stepped into the room, while Larry remained poised in the doorway. Although Jim may have sensed a presence behind his left shoulder, he waited at least another full second before turning his head....

It was more than enough time for Lyons.

Lyons struck low, moving in with a whipping kick to Jim's left knee. He then grabbed hold of the Texan's right arm and dropped his weight on the joint.

The bone snapped with an audible crack, and the Texan arched with an anguished scream. Larry spun, dropping to a crouch and swinging his Beretta in a long arc. But even as he drew a bead, Blancanales had launched into his own move. He began with a short side-step, while drawing back his right arm. Then he stepped to the left, letting the poker fly. The twenty-one inches of heavy brass turned once in the air before striking Larry's head—just below the right eye, leaving the stocky man stunned, motionless and blinded by a mess of blood.

Larry fired three shots as he sank to his knees, three wild shots that sent a spray of plaster off the walls. Before he could squeeze off a fourth, however, Blancanales was on him. He went for the back first, with a skipping snap-kick to the base of the spine. He then followed with a descending hammer-fist to the neck, and Larry dropped immediately.

Lyons quickly removed the .22 automatic from Jim's fingers, while Blancanales retrieved Larry's Beretta. For a moment the four men just looked at one another: the Texans sprawled on the shag and breathing through clenched teeth, Able Team carefully examining their newfound weapons.

"You boys still ain't going to make it," Jim said. His right arm was bent at an ugly angle, a jagged edge of bone exposed.

"That's right," Larry whispered from the depths of his own pain. "They ain't going to make it...no way, no how."

But by this time Lyons and Blancanales had already ripped out the phone cord, stepped into the passage and locked the door behind them. Pausing in the softly lit corridor to cock their weapons, they moved out.

13

"Any idea how you want to play it now?" Blancanales asked softly as the two men left the headquarters of the consortium.

Lyons quickly scanned the grounds around them. Although the sun still hung above the flat horizon, the sky above would soon be dark, the stars hidden by approaching cloud. He was also certain that the surrounding megaphones would soon be blaring out a screeching alarm.

"I think we'd better play it fast," he finally breathed. "I think we'd better get ourselves to that airstrip and play it real fast."

There were three vehicles parked along the edge of the executive offices: two stretch limousines and a Ford Bronco. Although the Bronco probably would have proved more effective for the long haul, Lyons finally decided on a limo. Not only would the fifty-five-thousand-dollar automobile offer them a little more authority, he decided, but it was ultimately faster than the Ford. The fact that the keys were dangling from its ignition also helped him make his choice.

"Maybe you should ride in back," Lyons said as he slipped behind the wheel. "Might buy us another couple of minutes if anyone stops us."

Blancanales slid into the back seat with a grin. "All right, James, let's go."

Lyons eased into reverse, then slowly pulled out along the frozen road. As they approached the main gates of the inner compound, he saw the uniformed guard speaking on a telephone and nodding. But it was not until he had been waved past the main gates that someone, probably one of the Texans, had finally managed to sound the alarm.

It was just under two miles from the consortium's executive compound to the airstrip—two miles of tundra disturbed only by a few storage tanks and gleaming pipes. As Lyons increased the pressure of his foot on the accelerator, he quickly assessed the situation: half a tank of gas, six .22 rounds, eight 9 mm rounds and two Ford Broncos bearing down hard.

"Tell me something," he said to Blancanales. "If you were Sweeny or Denton, what would be your next move?"

Blancanales glanced back through the rear window at the trailing Fords. "I guess that depends upon what sort of arrangement I had with the regular oil people," he replied. "I mean, if I was actually part of the main Prudhoe Bay group, I guess I'd cut my losses and run. Pretend that the whole thing was a big mistake and send out apologies with a case of cognac. If, on the other hand, I was an independent contractor hired to solve a local problem, I guess I'd be doing what they seem to be doing right now—trying to apprehend us."

"Yeah," Lyons agreed. "That's pretty much how I see it, although I think we both realize they're not going to be content at just catching us." Easing up on the accelerator to negotiate the last stretch of road before the airstrip, he withdrew the .22 from his parka and laid it on the seat.

From a distance the airstrip looked deserted. As Lyons brought the limousine closer, however, he caught a glimpse of two figures standing in the door of the corrugated hangar.

"This is how we play it," Lyons said as he pulled the limo to a stop beside the hangar. "We grab the first pilot that we see and tell him it's a case of fly or die."

"What if none of these guys are pilots?" Blancanales asked, slipping out of the limo and dropping the safety on his Beretta.

"Then it's still fly or die," Lyons answered.

They moved in a half crouch toward the hangar door. On the road behind them, the two Broncos were bearing down fast. Inside the hangar, however, it was strangely calm, with country music wafting from a portable radio and a television flickering in the corner. The slender boys in overalls and parkas were drinking cans of Coke, while a balding man in a flight jacket sipped whiskey from the bottle.

"You the pilot?" Lyons asked, the .22 now concealed in his pocket.

The balding man rose to his feet and nodded. "I'm the pilot, but I don't work for them public relations idiots. I work for myself—period. Besides, I ain't flying tonight, not with them mounting clouds out there."

Lyons glanced behind him through the half-open hangar door. The Ford Broncos were easing into the last turn, then braking hard as the doors flew open.

"What if I were to tell you that those clouds out there are nothing compared to the storm that's about to hit you right here and now?" Lyons asked.

The balding man ran a hand across his mouth. Then, catching sight of the .22 automatic in Lyons's hand, he simply smiled. "Well, in that case you can call me Al, and I am definitely your pilot."

Blancanales had moved to the hangar door during their exchange and had dropped to a crouch. Lyons, one hand now on the pilot's shoulder, moved in behind him. Beyond the door, across fifty yards of icy pavement, at least four men crouched behind the first Bronco. Blancanales pointed out a fifth man beneath the control tower, although Lyons thought it might have been a play of the Arctic's evening shadows.

"Now, I don't presume to tell you boys how to do your job," the pilot whispered. "But I do believe there may be an easier way to go about all this."

Lyons scanned the pavement ahead, calculating the distance between the two Broncos and the aircraft while trying to recall how long it took to get a six-seater into the sky. "I'm listening," he said.

"Well, just in case you boys still hold any illusions to the contrary, those fellows out there will most definitely start shooting the moment we show our pretty little faces."

"So?" Blancanales said, also attempting to calculate the distances, the time factor and the range.

"So we might stand a better chance if we slipped out the back door and picked us out a plane along the rear strip."

Lyons and Blancanales exchanged a quick glance. "The rear strip?" Lyons asked.

The pilot nodded past the mechanics to a narrow door at the opposite end of the hangar. "Yeah," he said. "The rear strip."

Six minutes later, after sprinting twenty yards through the chilled darkness, Lyons and Blancanales huddled beside the pilot in a twin-engine Beechcraft.

"Now, where did you fellows say you wanted to go?" the pilot drawled.

"Up," Lyons replied, his eyes fixed on two figures rounding the end of the hangar and leveling what looked like automatic rifles. "Up and away."

A burst of autofire cracked out from the hangar door as the Beechcraft's engines roared to life. A second burst shot from the darkness as the pilot swung the plane around and taxied out to the strip. There were echoes of at least two slugs slamming into the wings, but the pilot merely shook his head and grinned.

"Ain't nothing," he said.

There were two or three more bursts of autofire as the Beechcraft finally climbed into the air, shuddering in the chilled wind. There were no lights on the far horizon, no moon and no stars. There was only the seemingly endless expanse of tundra and dark ice beneath them.

"By the way," the pilot shouted over the drone of the straining engines. "What exactly did you boys do to piss them PR fellows off so much?"

"Good question," Lyons sighed, shifting his gaze to the terrible blackness below. "A very good question."

14

Gadgets Schwarz gazed out into the terrible blackness. What *do* we do if they come back before help arrives? he asked himself.

It was just after ten-thirty. Maggie Defoe had finally left the maps and was curled up on one of the narrow cots. Although the wind had not grown appreciably stronger, the ice fog had finally become impenetrable. And with the fog had come Maggie's question, "What do we do if they come back to kill us before help arrives?"

Gadgets stepped a little closer to the Plexiglas window adjacent to the door of the Quonset hut. Now and again, as the fingers of fog rose and curled, he briefly imagined seeing leaping wolf-men, hunched bear-men, advancing riflemen. There was also something vaguely disturbing about the sound of the wind through the chain-link fence and the whine of the rattling radio wires. But what ultimately bothered him the most was the fact that he had no answer to Maggie's question.

He moved back from the window and looked at the woman, now dozing on the cot. Although her shapeless parka and snow gear didn't do much for her figure, he thought that she was very beautiful. He also thought that he was starting to develop feelings for her.

He glanced at the deer rifle resting against his makeshift firing post, then slowly eased his right hand down until it rested on the butt of his automatic. He shifted his gaze to the cans of gasoline and pile of blankets, then back to the case of empty whiskey bottles. What do we do if they come back? There's only one thing to do, his mind screamed. We fight.

His weapons inventory complete, he decided it was time to wake Maggie up. He called her name softly and then gently placed a hand on her shoulder. "Come on, honey, it's time to get up."

She shook her head with a soft moan, then rose to an elbow and stared at him. "Is something wrong?"

He gave her a reassuring smile. "No, nothing's wrong. It's just time that we do some work."

He gave her his field knife and a blanket and told her to cut the heavy cotton into ten-inch squares. "And remember—" he grinned "—neatness counts." He then withdrew four empty whiskey bottles from the case in the corner, removed the cap from the gasoline can and fashioned a funnel from the cover of a *Playboy* magazine. As he filled the bottles with gasoline, his eye fell on a box of industrial tacks, and it briefly crossed his mind that he might be able to add a little shrapnel kick. But with the wind now screaming through the radio wires and clawing at the corrugated roof, he decided that there wasn't time.

As they completed their third incendiary device—a Wild Turkey bottle stopped with gasoline-soaked rags and candle wax—Gadgets became aware of the low moan of an engine.

He waited until the sound grew to a recognizable throb before extinguishing the lights and slipping into his parka. Withdrawing his .45 and handing it to Maggie, he offered another reassuring smile. "All you got to do is squeeze the trigger," he told her. "Hang on tight and squeeze the trigger."

She took the weapon, testing the weight of it and its feel. "Why do you have to go back out there?" she asked, her voice now clearly laced with fear. "Why can't you stay here?"

He hefted the deer rifle over his shoulder. "Because out there they won't be able to see me."

He smiled at her from the doorway and then told her to draw the bolt behind him.

The first breath of air was like a knife in his throat and brought tears to his eyes. But by the time he reached the shadow of the radio tower, he was actually starting to feel pretty good... mean and hard.

From his position below the tower, he was able to see only forty or fifty feet beyond the chain-link fence. Beyond that point there was nothing but a black curtain of swirling fog. And then, from the corner of his eye, he caught the quick sweep of headlights from at least two approaching vehicles.

He slipped the deer rifle from his shoulder, chambered the first cartridge and hunkered down beside the steel beam. Although the lights had vanished, the rumble of the engines was unmistakable. They're testing us, he told himself. They're slowly circling the perimeter to draw us out.

He rose to a crouch again and began moving forward on the balls of his feet. Twenty yards in front of the main gate were four stacked oil barrels and a low drainage ditch. After briefly pausing by the barrels, he slipped into the ditch and fixed the rifle sight at sixty yards. He wished he had an infrared or even a pair of night-vision goggles with him.

But even as this thought passed through his mind, his eyes were beginning to fix on a figure—squat and hooded and slowly materializing out of the fog.

The ditch was littered with discarded junk, the legacy of former soldiers. There were empty soup cans, whiskey bottles and literally hundreds of burnt Sterno cans. Slowly inching his gloved fingers across the cold concrete, he even encountered the antlers of a caribou. Finally closing his hand around something hard and cylindrical, he picked up a nine-inch piece of lead pipe.

He hesitated before tossing the pipe. Then, catching another glimpse of the enemy in the fog, he hurled the pipe hard and high onto the roof of the radio shack. It impacted on the corrugated iron with a hollow clang, like a bucket falling from the rafters of an empty warehouse.

The man froze before responding. He dropped to a crouch and turned with a fast, blind burst of autofire.

Okay, Schwarz realized, so he's a bag guy. Bad guy, because only bad guys shoot without asking questions.

The Able Team warrior dropped to his belly, moving slowly over the trash-littered floor of the drainage ditch. Should have brought a grenade launcher, he told himself—and a ski mask, because the wind was cutting his nose and lips, cutting like razor ice.

He caught a glimpse of three more figures running out of the fog. Like the first, they appeared to be armed with CAR-15s, which meant that they were professionals. The locals didn't use weapons like that. They moved low and fast and seemed to have an extremely keen sense of how one fought in this forsaken place.

But they did not know that Schwarz was watching them.

He picked up a second fragment of pipe from the litter, waited a moment, then hurled it in a high arc to his left. A moment later he heard the hollow echo of lead against iron. Then came another rapid burst of 5.56 mm ammunition as the third and fourth hooded figures let loose with their CAR-15s. It was followed by a second or two of ringing silence, then his own first shot.

He remained on his belly, sighting through the chain-link and holding his breath as he fired. He aimed for the chest because he couldn't be sure about the head, not with the tendrils of fog and the wind. He saw the hooded figure stumble before he fell, saw the man wavering for a moment in dull surprise. After a couple of awkward steps, the figure simply sank to the ground and lay there.

More blind bursts of autofire rang across the compound, the hot slugs pounding into corrugated metal and glancing off the radio tower. Someone shouted in terror or rage, and there were echoes of a rumbling engine again.

Schwarz had slipped between two storage tanks and then into the black mouth of a six-foot sewage pipe. He felt safe, calm, more in control.

He took four slow, deep breaths and mentally willed himself to stop shivering. It was no use. He carefully laid down the deer rifle, rose to a squat and tried rubbing his legs. It made too much noise. He pressed a gloved hand to his face and gently massaged his nose and mouth before picking up the rifle again, and easing himself back to the ice-encrusted mouth of the drainage pipe. To hell with the cold, he thought.

There were footsteps now, a soft and easy tread of steps just beyond the chain-link fence. And there were more lights, two long columns of yellow light probing the ditch and the shadows of the radio tower. Then, as if out of nowhere, four hooded figures looked directly at him from less than thirty feet away.

He pressed himself down to the icy surface of the drainage pipe, praying that their eyes couldn't penetrate the blackness. He felt the shock of cold stab into his cheek and a burning cramp in his leg. At the same time, he heard the unmistakable click of a bolt-assisted closing mechanism that differentiated the CAR-15 XM177 from the XM 177-E1, and he knew that he couldn't wait a second longer.

Gadgets fired as the first hooded figure dropped to his knee. He fired for the chest again, because it was the cleanest shot. The figure rose as if kicked by a mule, then dropped in a heap. He was replaced immediately; a second man began squeezing off a burst of fire.

Eight slugs screamed into the mouth of the drain, glancing off the steel in a spray of icy sparks. Schwarz rolled, scampering on hands and knees deeper into the darkness as a second burst sent another volley of slugs above his head. He felt something impact with his shoulder and felt the blood drain from his face. But he'd only hit the joint of the pipe, a protruding slab of welded steel where the drain curved still deeper into the blackness.

Gadgets stood still. Judging from the stench, he supposed that he was in some sort of septic tank but was definitely still above ground. He was also fairly certain that less than twenty yards beyond the lip of the tank lay the Quonset hut where Maggie waited—alone in the darkness and obviously terrified.

He slid out of the tank, first peering over the lip, then slithering down to the cold ground. There were two yellow beams of light now probing the compound, one atop the Jeep, the other probably hand held. There were more enemy recruits, at least a few men carrying automatic rifles.

He hesitated for about fifteen seconds before crossing the final thirty feet to the Quonset hut. Although he may have been able to drop at least one figure along the rim of the compound, he couldn't risk exposing his position, not now, not so close to Maggie's position. So he simply waited: watching, listening and shivering in the biting chill. He knew there were at least two more figures probing the edge of the perimeter, two more determined killers in hooded parkas and face masks.

He waited another eight or nine seconds before rising to his feet and moving out again. He kept low, skirting the shadows of the dormitory and fixing his gaze on the ground in front of him. When he finally reached the door of the hut, he gently knocked twice before whispering, "It's me."

"THEY KNOW WE'RE here, don't they?" Maggie asked softly, her voice unsteady, her shoulders trembling.

He sank to the cot, pressing a finger to his numbed lips. "Not yet," he replied.

She brought him a flask of Wild Turkey and told him to sip it very slowly. She also brought him a blanket she had warmed with her body and told him to press it to his face. Then, probably because she was frightened, Maggie gently laid her head on his shoulder and shut her eyes.

"What are we going to do?" she asked quietly.

He glanced at the misted square of Plexiglas that seemed to float in the blackness above the bolted door. "Keep them guessing," he said. "We're going to keep them guessing."

He rose from the cot, picked up a coil of electrical wire and a faintly glowing kerosene lamp. Threading his way through the darkness until his fingers encountered the door, he dropped to one knee. Adjusting the lamp so that the glow of light extended no more than six inches into the blackness, he carefully set it down in front of the door. Next, securing an end of the wire to a leg of a cot, he slowly picked his way back through the darkness to the opposite end of the hut. There he probed again in the blackness until his fingers encountered the loose sheet of paneling that would serve as their escape hatch. Finally, attaching the wire to the loose panel of sheet metal, he felt his way back to Maggie.

He saw only her outline in the blackness, a trembling shadow against the darker shadows.

"Are we ready?" she asked softly.

He took her hand and placed it on the taut wire he had attached to the loose panel at the rear of the hut. "Things start getting too heavy," he whispered, "you just follow this wire to safety. You understand?"

"What about you?"

He laid his hand on top of hers and smiled. "I'll be right behind you."

And then the waiting game began. For a long time, at least ten or fifteen minutes, there was only the sound of the wind. Now and again it sounded almost human, like a softly moaning child. Then suddenly the sounds changed and grew closer.

Schwarz felt the girl's hand clutch his shoulder, but he ignored her. There were sounds of something moving along the side of the hut, then something actually tugging at the doorknob. Schwarz lifted the deer rifle, dropped the safety and sighted above the glow of the lamp he had left on the floor. Then he waited.

"Be very quiet," he whispered to Maggie. "No matter what happens, just be quiet."

But when the door finally burst open, she couldn't entirely suppress her scream.

Schwarz waited until the first intruder hit the trip wire and tumbled onto a cot before he fired. Sighting into the glow of the kerosene lamp, he squeezed off one shot and hit the chest of the second intruder.

There was a long burst of 5.56 mm fire as the stricken figure staggered, reeling back out into the night. It was followed by a second burst as the first intruder rose to his knees and sprayed a dozen wild rounds into the blackness. But by this time Schwarz had begun to squeeze off his second shot, a second big round from his 336-CS Marlin.

The kneeling man seemed to shiver before he fell, a brief spasmodic shiver as a cloud of blood rose from the top of his skull. He screamed, but it was lost in the crack of additional fire from the door.

Schwarz felt Maggie trembling beside him, felt fragments of steel raining into his hair. He heard another eight or nine 5.56 mm rounds slam into the steel cabinets, then finally laid down the Marlin and took his .45 auto from her hand.

They're firing blind, he told himself. They still don't know where we are, so they're firing blind from just outside the door. But when he rose above the filing cabinets, extending the .45 in his stiff right arm, at least nine rounds slammed into the panel above his head.

He aimed at the muzzle-flash, squeezed off three fast rounds at what he hoped was a torso. He saw the muzzle-flash waver as yet another scream tore out of the blackness, then dropped for cover as eight or nine more heavy slugs exploded around him.

Maggie began whimpering beside him. There was a whine of slugs glancing off the floorboards, and the filing cabinets suddenly started bucking with the impact of more hot lead.

Schwarz jammed the .45 between his knees, reached for a kerosene-filled whiskey bottle and withdrew his butane lighter. Something hard and sharp sliced across his left wrist, but he ignored it. Another burst of autofire cut into the filing cabinets, filling Schwarz's ears with the clatter of shattering metal. But by now he had actually managed to light the fuse, and rolling back on his haunches, he let it fly.

He tossed the flaming bottle with an enraged cry as the slugs continued to clatter around him. There may have been a cry of warning from the doorway, but it was lost in the screams.

The flames shot out in two long tongues, the first rising to lick the rafters, the second pouring out the doorway in a crackling sheet. There were shouts of terror and a brief glimpse of a figure slamming himself against the doorjamb. Then came another wild burst of autofire, but by this time Schwarz had already started moving.

"Let's go," he whispered to the girl. Placing her hand on the guide wire that would lead them through the blackness to the rear of the cot, he repeated himself, "Let's go, honey. Let's go."

He squeezed another three rounds from his modified .45 auto as he moved out from behind the barricade of filing cabinets. As flames spread inward to an upturned cot, long tongues of light momentarily illuminated the interior of the hut and left him outlined in the darkness—as clean a target as anyone could ask for. But before another spray of autofire poured through the doorway, Gadgets squeezed off three more rounds and found himself once again in relative darkness.

The Able Team warrior knew it was only about twenty-five feet from the filing cabinets to the end of the hut where he'd created his escape hatch. Although the flames from the doorway threw a little light across the floor, the ends of the hut were still pitch-black. Now and again Schwarz caught glimpses of Maggie as she followed the wire in a low crouch.

When he reached the hatch, he had to feel for the loose panel of corrugated steel as another random burst of autofire poured in from the doorway.

"Once you get outside," he whispered to Maggie, "start running for the fog bank and don't stop for anything."

"What about you?"

"I'll be right behind you."

He finally had to kick the panel out by sitting on the floor and repeatedly driving the heel of his boot into the corrugated steel in order to clear a passage. And even then it was tight, hardly enough room for Maggie's shoulders.

"Go!" he ordered, shoving her through the narrow slit in the side of the hut. *Go!*

More autofire sprayed through the doorway from the opposite end of the hut, at least sixteen blind rounds, slamming off the floor. He briefly considered tossing a second incendiary bottle, but finally decided that there simply wasn't time. So, after emptying the last of his .45 clip and sliding the deer rifle through, he dived to his belly and started forward.

The edges of his escape hatch were jagged, and his parka kept snagging on daggers of steel. He also had difficulty slipping his left shoulder through the narrow passage and finally had to let go of the kerosene bottle. But it wasn't until he was halfway out—head and shoulders in the chilled air, legs still inside the hut—that he realized he would probably never make it.

The autofire had stopped. Then he heard what sounded like a labored grunt and what may have been the quick breath of a dog. Gadgets thought he also heard the sound of claws on the floorboards and the frenzied snarl of a ravenous beast.

Schwarz couldn't suppress a howl of pain as something bit into the calf of his leg. He couldn't keep himself from arching back with a shivering scream as something tore into his flesh and ripped it away.

He twisted, frantically kicking at the thing. He felt something hard and bony and definitely not human. And then his thoughts turned only to the searing pain.

Noooooo! he cried.

He saw Maggie turn back in horror at the sound of his voice, saw her ash-white face in the coils of fog and her slender hands reach out to him.

But there was nothing she could do to help him now, not with the fangs sinking deeper and deeper.

"Run!" he screamed. "Maggie, run!"

But she kept coming closer, stumbling down to her knees and reaching for the deer rifle.

He felt the teeth sink into his knee, possibly all the way to the bone. He heard another enraged snarl and thought that the thing wasn't killing—it was feeding.

He felt the teeth dig in again, felt the head thrash back and forth in a hungered frenzy. He turned on his side to kick it again and caught a glimpse of its massive head—gray and elongated. Only its eyes were human. Then came more searing pain, and he was finally conscious of nothing except the deafening crack of the Marlin.

Maggie squeezed off two rounds into the corrugated siding. Then, cocking and ejecting as quickly as she could, she squeezed off three more shells toward the thrashing shadows.

Schwarz heard what might have been a squeal of pain, then felt the pressure of jaws subside. He twisted on his hip, furiously kicking until he finally felt his legs slip free. Frantically reaching for Maggie's outstretched hand, he finally dragged himself through the hole.

Gadgets was mainly conscious of the little things. He was conscious of the numbing pain in his shredded leg and what felt like a bone exposed to the icy air. He was conscious of the undulating fog, like a vast and protective wall around him. The Able Team warrior was also conscious of the dim but frantic voices behind him and the sporadic shots from within the hut. But mostly he was conscious of Maggie, still clutching his hand and urging him on, deeper and deeper into the frozen wastes.

15

"Want a little advice?" the pilot had asked Lyons and Blancanales as he'd landed the plane in the darkness. "Get your butts out of here, and fast. You get what I'm saying? Them ol' boys from Prudhoe Bay are not about to let you get away with this. So if I were you, I'd get myself out of the state, and fast."

But as they stood shivering on the edge of the strip and gazed out to shore-fast ice, it occurred to Lyons that the ball was now in Able Team's court.

"Maybe we'd better check in on Gadgets," Blancanales finally suggested. "See how he's doing out there."

Lyons merely shrugged with an indifferent sigh. "Sure," he answered, and the two men began to trek to their hotel.

When Blancanales first requested the use of the shortwave radio, a sleepy woman behind the desk told him to go to hell. But then something in the stranger's eyes and the tone of his voice eventually convinced the woman to indulge her guest.

Lyons was facing the window when Blancanales finally emerged from the radio room. Although one or two natives who were lounging in the lobby had briefly noted his presence, no one had bothered him.

"I can't reach them," Blancanales said softly. "I can't even get a whisper."

Lyons shifted his gaze from the window to a plastic clock above the door. "Maybe they're sleeping," he said. "Maybe they're—" He broke off with a shake of his head.

"Point is, I think we'd better get out there. I think we'd better get out there right now."

Lyons returned his gaze to the blue wastes of ice beyond the window, to the wall of white fog still moving in from the east and the strange glow of the sun along the horizon. Turning to Blancanales, he said, "All I can say, ol' buddy, is you'd better not be wrong about this."

IT WAS EXACTLY midnight when Lyons and Blancanales finally began driving along the coastal road. Fog, which still lay in patches around the community, soon grew very thick.

"It's a feeling, okay?" Blancanales said, breaking the silence between the two. "I got a feeling that something's wrong."

"Nothing wrong with going with your gut," Lyons replied. "I'm just having a little trouble imagining what they could do to Gadgets that he couldn't handle. Not to mention the fact that they'd have a pretty hard time finding him."

"You think so?" Blancanales countered. "Well, ponder this for a moment. They'd know from the flight manifests that no plane left the Barrow strip. They'd also realize that Gadgets and Maggie Defoe would probably stay in commuting range of us. You add that all together and then take a look at a map, and I think you'd be able to pinpoint their location pretty easily."

Although Lyons did not actually say anything, his right foot pressed down a little harder on the accelerator.

They did not see the compound until they were virtually on top of it, and even then they could make out only the faintest outlines of the structures: the sagging dormitory, the corrugated hut, the radio tower and the shed. Lyons pulled the Jeep to a stop but kept the engine running. Blancanales withdrew his Marlin from the back of the cab, chambered a round and released the safety.

"No lights," he said softly. "You see that? There are no lights."

"Yeah," Lyons breathed, also reaching for his deer rifle. "I see it."

They climbed out of the Jeep, then slowly started tramping toward the main gate. Now and again the wind cut swathes through the fog and offered glimpses of a door swinging on its hinges. But Lyons did not say anything until he drew closer.

"Gadgets is tough," Lyons said softly, as much to himself as to Blancanales. "I mean, that guy is one tough bastard. I remember one time in Vegas..."

But by this time they had passed the main gate and were moving into the compound where the first two bodies still lay curled on the cold gravel. They saw the tire tracks left by a vehicle, a scattering of automatic shells and the scorched entrance of the Quonset hut where they had last seen Gadgets and Maggie.

Blancanales withdrew a flashlight and slowly inspected the faces of the fallen men. He knelt on one knee for a futile examination of their pockets, then rose again to sweep the beam of light across the grounds, searching for an explanation of what had gone down.

They approached the entrance of the Quonset cautiously, following the line of the flashlight until it fell on the huddled forms of the third and fourth bodies in the doorway. For a moment, Lyons thought the men were still breathing. Then he saw the ragged holes from Schwarz's .45 and simply shook his head.

Good for you buddy, he thought. Good for you.

After another quick and pointless examination of the bodies, Blancanales swept the flashlight beam in a wide arc to reveal the wide spacing of bullet holes, the makeshift firing post of filing cabinets, the upturned cots, the trip wires and blackened glass.

"There must have been at least six or seven of them," Blancanales said at last. "At least six or seven coming right at him."

"That doesn't mean anything," Lyons countered. "It doesn't mean a damn thing."

But by this time Blancanales had trained the flashlight beam on the spots of blood behind the filing cabinet and the ragged holes from the fully automatic rifles.

"Figure it this way," he said. "Denton and Sweeny get word that Maggie and Gadgets were waiting for us out here. They figure they can catch two birds with one stone with a team of local mercs. But the team doesn't want to wait it out in the cold forever. So they decide to hell with it and they move in on Gadgets with everything they've got."

Lyons sank to the cot, his tired gaze now fixed on the barricade of filing cabinets, on the three or four shells from Gadgets's automatic. "I still don't see it," he said at last.

"Then what?" Blancanales asked. "Huh? Tell me what you see?"

Lyons shook his head, his gaze now shifting to the taut line of electrical wire that Schwarz had strung across the length of the hut.

"I'm not sure," he said softly. "But what if—" He broke off and rose to his feet again. Then, removing his left mitten, he bent to examine the fragments of a whiskey bottle at his feet.

"Look at it this way," he continued, picking up a shard of blackened glass. "First he tries to torch them. He holds his fire to suck them inside, then tosses a bottle of kerosene in their faces."

"Which slows them down for about four minutes—max," Blancanales put in.

"But that's all he needs. He only needs three or four minutes of confusion in order to make his next move."

"Which is?"

Lyons extended a hand to the taut length of electrical wire. "It's dark, right?" he said softly, still fingering the wire. "Even though there are flames at the door, it's still pretty dark in here. Shadows dancing all over the walls, autofire spraying everywhere. Major confusion. But Gadgets had figured on all of that, right? He's planned for it, and that's why he'd got this wire strung from his firing post to his escape hatch. It's his lifeline, and all he's got to do is follow it."

"But Maggie goes first, right?"

Lyons nodded. "Sure, she goes first, but the main thing is that he's moving. He's moving at a pretty good clip."

"And the guys at the door?"

Lyons shrugged, rising to his feet and then slowly following the wire to the rear of the room. "They still haven't figured out what's going on," he said. "They're fighting fire at this point, so they really..." He bent down to inspect the ragged slit in the side of the hut where Schwarz had torn his escape hatch. "They really don't have a clue."

Blancanales trained the flashlight on the jagged edge of corrugated steel, on the empty .45 shells and the fragments of another whiskey bottle. Then very slowly, bringing the light a little closer, he saw the blood, the bits of torn nylon and finally a fragment of gray fur.

The Able Team warrior dropped to a knee, picked up the clump of animal fur and examined it in the light. "I think it must have gotten him as he was crawling through," he said softly. "He's got his head and shoulders out the hatch, and all of sudden it's on him."

Lyons also dropped to a knee, but his eyes were examining the blood. "But that still doesn't mean he didn't make it. They release the animal, or whatever the hell it is. The thing comes in like a hound from hell and takes a few bites out of Gadgets's leg. He's hurting and he's worried, but he's not giving up, no way."

"So what's your point?"

Lyons hunkered down still lower, inching his head through the ragged hole until he finally had a vision of what lay beyond: the mess of bootprints, the patches of blood, the shells from the Marlin and then the fog.

"My point," he said at last, "is that they're still out there. Gadgets may be hurting because some damn wolf-man took a hunk out of his leg, but he's got Maggie and they're still out there."

Blancanales leaned forward for a better view of what lay beyond. "I guess Gadgets figured he would try to lose them in the fog," he said. "I guess he figured that the time had come to run for it."

"Which means that we'd better find them before Sweeny and Denton's people find them," Lyons said.

"Or before that...that *thing* finds them," Blancanales added, his eyes now fixed on the four-pad print in the dirt.

16

The fog was moving in from the northeast, and Schwarz knew that they shouldn't head in that direction.

"How's your leg?" Maggie asked when they finally paused to catch their breath.

Schwarz gingerly probed his lacerated thigh and calf. "It's fine, just fine," he said, although as he peeled away a layer of blood-drenched wool, he couldn't entirely suppress a grimace.

It was difficult for Schwarz to tell exactly where they were. Barely visible in the fog, beyond a rock outcrop there appeared to be some sort of man-made structure—possibly a weather station or another deserted radio tower. Gadgets thought he occasionally heard the sounds of vehicles on some unseen road, although it may have only been jostling ice sheets in the spring thaw.

"We're in trouble, aren't we?" Maggie asked after another long pause. "We're up a creek without a paddle, aren't we?"

Schwarz grew very still at the echo of what he thought was an approaching truck, but then finally shook his head with a quick, hard grin. "Trouble? This isn't trouble. This is fun."

His lacerated leg was beginning to cramp in the cold, and he didn't like the feel of the tendon whenever he tried to flex his knee.

They began moving again, struggling over patches of soil and hummocks of lichen. Then came a long stretch of candled ice and frozen earth. Once or twice Schwarz was certain he heard the drone of a vehicle probing the fog bank behind them, but he saw no point in even glancing back over his shoulder.

He paused again at the base of a cone-shaped mound of blue ice covered with a mantle of lichen and tufted Arctic grass.

"Tell me something," Schwarz panted, resting his weight on his good leg. "What do the Eskimo do when they're lost on the ice?"

Maggie laid down the Marlin and sank to her haunches. "Eskimo don't get lost on the ice," she said.

"Come on, it must happen. What if some Eskimo was out hunting on the floe, and all of a sudden the ice breaks up and he starts drifting out to sea. What would the guy do?"

She shook her head with a deep sigh and shifted her gaze to the gray wastes ahead. "He'd get on his radio and call a helicopter," she said.

Beyond the vegetated frost heave, lay another barren stretch of scattered ice and frozen tundra. The ground was frozen, and Schwarz found himself continually sliding on patches of ice, continually staggering over slippery lichen. He was also certain that his leg was bleeding again. But having caught another echo of an engine on the breeze, he didn't stop to check.

The fog grew thicker as they neared the shore, the air colder. The echo of the engines was also louder. Someone was definitely trying to follow them.

And then Schwarz saw the slow sweep of a spotlight.

He dragged Maggie down to the ground and took the deer rifle out of her hands. Slowly peering above the humped mounds of barren soil, he saw it again: the penetrating yellow beam of a mounted spotlight.

"How did they find us?" Maggie whispered. "How the hell did they find us in this fog?"

Maybe the wolf-man can smell us, Schwarz thought. "I don't know," was all he said.

He rolled on his side to cock the Marlin, grimacing again as the ice granules seeped into his wound. Six rounds, he thought. Three rounds in the Marlin and three rounds in the .45. Then, briefly shutting his eyes in pain, he suddenly recalled the feel of the fangs in his flesh and the stench of the wolf-man's breath. And just in case, he told himself, I've got to save a round for Maggie and a round for me to end things quickly and painlessly.

The throb of the engine seemed to grow steadier and Schwarz realized that the Jeep had finally stopped. He caught the sound of doors closing and voices.

And then he heard the frenzied whine of a hungry wolf.

"But I shot it," Maggie whispered in disbelief. "I shot the damn thing."

Schwarz laid a hand on her shoulder to steady her. "It's not real," he told her softly. "It's just some kind of a trick, that's all."

But as another maddened howl reverberated out of the fog, Maggie just shook her head. "I don't think you understand," she said. "Some of those old legends are based in reality. Some of those old Eskimo really do have powers. I've seen it with my own eyes."

Schwarz did not respond—he was too busy watching dark forms move across the fog-shrouded landscape.

He hefted the deer rifle, adjusting the sight for a hundred yards before dropping the safety. I should have brought something with a flash suppressor, he told himself. Maybe even a silencer.

Three ghostly figures now moved in a ragged line out of the mist. They were followed by some sort of man-beast.

He felt Maggie's hand clutch his arm again, heard her soft moan of terror. I'll take it with a chest shot, he told himself. I'll cut right through the chest and go for the vital organs. But he also knew that the greatest danger still lay with the men, with their fully automatic CAR-15s and whatever the hell else they were packing.

Gadgets waited until he could actually see the outline of their weapons, until he could hear the crunch of their boots on the frozen ground. Then, sighting on the front man, lining up the cross hairs with the dark features beneath the hood, he slowly squeezed the trigger.

The front man staggered before he fell. The impact left him momentarily stunned, as if suddenly struck in the face with a rock. Staggering back in a cloud of hot blood, he crumpled into a heap amid the tufts of Arctic grass.

Five rounds left.

There were inarticulate cries, and someone shouted, "He's over there!" The long beam of yellow light immediately cut out from the base of the frost heave, and then the inevitable bursts of autofire racked across the tundra.

Schwarz pressed Maggie's shoulders to the ice-crusted mud. "We've got to move out to the shore."

She nodded, meeting his gaze. "What if..."

"Just do what I tell you, and everything will be all right."

He waited until the beam from the searchlight had passed beyond the rows of candled ice, then slowly hefted the Marlin again. Although one of the figures had vanished, the other was clearly visible: a crouching rifleman scanned the landscape with a pair of binoculars. He'll catch us the moment we start moving, Schwarz told himself. He'll spray a burst right into our backs the moment we rise.... And if that doesn't do it, he thought bitterly, he'll send in that damn creature.

Another minute passed. There was a shout from an unseen figure to his left. He knew it was now or never....

And sighting for the rifleman's heart, he squeezed off round two.

The big slug caught the man in the chest, picked him up and tossed him to the ground onto a patch of black lichen. But no sooner had he fallen than a second and third figure materialized out of the mist.

Gadgets rolled on his side, chambered the last shell and sighted for the figure descending the frost heave. He fired for the muzzle-flash, saw the man stagger in a ragged circle and sag to his knees. The Able Team warrior tossed away the Marlin and withdrew his .45 auto.

"Time to move out," he said to Maggie. "You with me, honey? Time to go," he repeated when she didn't respond.

She gave a dull and hopeless smile, then reached for his hand and nodded. "Sure, I'm with you."

Another figure had materialized out of the mist, and another eight or nine rounds from a CAR-15 cut into the candled ice. But having finally dragged Maggie to her feet, Schwarz had already started moving out. He moved at a half run, leading Maggie by her hand and ignoring the stabbing pain in his leg. He fixed his eyes on the faint humps of shore-fast ice and prayed that the fog would wrap them in a dense cocoon.

They were about sixty yards from the shore when Schwarz heard the throb of the engine and caught another glimpse of the searchlight. Someone shouted a name, and then he heard the scream of tires over frost-layered rock. Gadgets dragged Maggie back down to the ground.

They sank between rows of candled ice and a low ridge of glacier-smoothed rock. Schwarz dropped the safety on his automatic but still didn't let go of Maggie's hand. Although there were still echoes of activity all around them, nothing was visible through the fog.

"We're in trouble, aren't we?" Maggie whispered, her frightened eyes turned up to Schwarz, her shoulders slightly trembling.

Schwarz met her gaze for a lingering moment, then nodded with a smile. "Yeah, we're in trouble."

"So what are we going to do?"

He shook his head. "I'm not sure."

There were three or four minutes of absolute silence before Schwarz finally heard them coming. The wind had died, the ice had ceased shifting and the throbbing engine had stopped. But from just beyond the edge of visible tundra, they heard the soft crunch of footsteps on frozen soil and the dark panting of a wolf.

Schwarz sank to his belly and told Maggie to assume the same position. Although his leg continued to ache, the pain became secondary as he thought of his three remaining rounds and the four figures making their way toward them.

He cocked the automatic and took a deep breath as the first two figures appeared out of the swirling grayness. He felt Maggie slide closer, then felt the pressure of her head on his shoulder. The first hooded figure grew steadily more defined, and Gadgets slowly shifted his arms until the man was in his firing line. But then he suddenly caught sight of four additional figures—including the beast—and he simply lowered his weapon and stared.

The creature was larger than he had imagined; it was at least a hundred and fifty pounds. And it didn't move exactly like an animal, but like some sort of ape. It paused to sniff the air before advancing, then paused again to listen. Finally rearing up on two legs, it threw back its head and howled.

Schwarz raised his weapon again, left hand bracing the right, elbows firmly planted on the rock. He felt Maggie tremble, and he softly urged her to be still, to shut her eyes and be still.

He was surprised at how relaxed he felt as he measured the distance, weighed the odds and wondered if there was any possibility of escape. The Able Team warrior finally decided that if he accomplished nothing else, he would at least take the beast out with him.

That decision made, he lifted the .45 again and sighted down the barrel.

The beast approached slowly, moving with a strangely awkward gait. At times it seemed to walk on four legs, at others on only two. Its breath left a ragged mist in the air, and its head kept shifting from side to side, but Schwarz aimed only at its chest. If it breathes, he told himself, then it has lungs, and if it has lungs, I can kill it. I can bring it down with one clean shot and still have two rounds left.

But even as he squeezed off that first shot, pressing his elbows in tight to steady his hands, he knew that it was hopeless.

He fired when the beast was only twenty yards away. The beast reared with the impact and then fell to its haunches. But just as suddenly as it fell, it was up again, teeth bared and howling.

Schwarz steadied his hands again with another deep breath. He heard Maggie whimpering beside him and he thought that if it didn't go down with this shot, he'd put the last bullet through her head. Gadgets sighted down the barrel, watched the creature fill his vision and then squeezed off the second shot.

The impact of the .45 swung the beast entirely around, left it briefly suspended before tossing it back down to the earth. But although it yelped in pain, it started to rise again, digging in with its rear legs and lurching forward.

He steadied the weapon for a third shot, knowing that it was hopeless, knowing that in thirty seconds the beast would be on them, tearing and ripping until there was nothing left but two heaps of shredded flesh. Maggie whimpered beside him, softly mouthing his name. Gadgets pulled her closer with his left hand, turned the muzzle of the .45 to her temple and told himself to do it. Put a bullet in her head, before that thing is on her!

But even as he started to squeeze the trigger, something told him to wait, to wait until the unearthly roaring stopped.

The sound brought everything to a halt: the beast, the crouching riflemen, even the probing searchlight. For an instant Schwarz thought it came from below him, from deep within the permafrost. Yet as the sound built with intensity, he realized that it came from behind him, from the edge of the shoreline, where at least a dozen ghostly figures had appeared.

A second ear-shattering roar broke from the shore, and the wolf-man seemed to waver, shaking its head and backing off. One of the crouched figures shouted something, let loose with a quick burst of autofire, then also started to retreat. In response to the CAR-15, eight rifle shots rang out from the fog. But by the time a third hollow roar had echoed into the sky, the ground ahead was deserted.

Schwarz slowly rose to his knees, peering through the layers of shifting fog. Although the figures still remained only faintly visible, he was able to make out their general build: short, stocky and obviously at home on the ice.

Eskimo? he wondered.

"Eskimo, Gadgets. They're Eskimo," Maggie whispered as if she'd read his thoughts. "They're Eskimo!" she repeated as she rose to her feet and began waving her arms.

But it wasn't until Schwarz had seen the broad, dark faces break into a smile that he finally lowered his weapon. He watched as they slowly approached, tramping across the ice with short, stiff steps. They walked in a ragged line, their rifles slung over their shoulders, the hoods of their parkas thrown back. Four or five dogs followed in their wake, one of them dragging a slaughtered seal. Heading the group was a strangely wizened little man with the trace of a mustache on his upper lip and very bright eyes. He had an odd, almost waltzing way of walking. Some fifteen feet away from them he stopped to face Schwarz and Maggie with his head cocked to the side.

"Hey, you want some Nescafé or not?"

Schwarz glanced at his companion, waited for her nod and then smiled. "Sure," he said. "Nescafé would be just great."

17

It was just about dawn when Gadgets and Maggie climbed out of the walrus-skin boat and onto the shores of the Eskimo encampment. Although the fog had moved off, the horizon was still obscure and the light remained faint and gray. From the water the encampment had looked like nothing more than a sprinkling of brown shacks tossed up by the tide. They quickly realized that the encampment was actually a small village, with a ragged row of frame houses two hundred yards from the sea. In contrast to the traditional sod, the houses were wood-shingled and sided with asphalt. A couple of them had even been fitted with television antennae.

Apparently it had been decided that the old man was to serve as host. His name, he told Schwarz, was Piitkaq, although many called him Pete. His wife's name was Sook, although Schwarz could call her Charlene. His house consisted of two cramped rooms, partially floored with linoleum. A yellow Formica table had been set in the kitchen, and there was a beanbag chair in the sitting room. There was also an old bentwood rocker, a battery-powered television set and a pedal-operated sewing machine. The washroom facilities consisted of a honey bucket, and the food was cooked on a camp stove.

"So," the old man said as Schwarz and Maggie entered the narrow passage, "what do you think? Pretty modern, huh?"

Schwarz wearily ran his eyes from a collection of cocktail glasses etched with the logos of National Football League teams to the skull of a bowhead embedded in the floor by the entrance.

"Yeah." He smiled. "It's pretty modern."

Coffee laced with whiskey was served, and the old man's wife withdrew a first-aid kit in order to attend to Schwarz's leg.

"So you two got into a little scrap, huh?" the old man said when his wife had peeled back Schwarz's makeshift bandage to reveal the wound.

Schwarz nodded, gritting his teeth as the woman began dabbing the wound with disinfectant. "Yeah," he sighed. "I guess you could say that's what happened."

"Well, that's the problem with the ice these days," the old man said. "There are all kinds of bad things running around out there. All kinds of things that will take a big bite out of you if you don't watch out."

Charlene had begun cleaning the clotted bits of wool from Schwarz's wound, while Maggie continued shivering over her coffee. They heard snatches of voices from the lane outside and the distant throb of rock music on a portable radio. At the same time, however, there were also echoes of someone singing an ancient and tuneless song.

"We're not from Fairbanks or Anchorage," Maggie said last. "We're from back east, from Washington."

"We're also not with the oil companies," Schwarz added.

Old Pete nodded. "Hey, I know that. You don't think I know that? That's why we saved you. That's why I scared those men away with my bear shout, okay?"

"Your bear shout?" Maggie asked, turning to look at him and suddenly growing very still.

"That's right, my bear shout." The old man smiled. "You heard it, didn't you? Loudest thing in the world. Louder and more frightening than the sound of a big oil truck—or a wolf."

Schwarz had grown very still and was now watching the old man's eyes. "And where did you learn it?" he asked. "Where?"

The Eskimo shook his head with another smile. "Where do you think I learned it? I learned it from a bear!"

"Tell us about the skinwalker, Pete," Maggie said, changing the conversation. "Tell us about the skinwalker out on the ice."

The old man tilted his head to one side and spread his lips in another smile. "Skinwalkers, huh? Who said there's any such thing as a skinwalker?"

Schwarz exchanged another quick glance with Maggie, then gently lifted his now-bandaged leg. "I say there's skinwalkers." He grinned. "Me and this here chewed-up leg."

The old Eskimo let his smile broaden slightly, then softly chuckled. "Well, in that case I guess we'd better have a little more of this whiskey and then I'll tell you what I've heard. Not that I believe a word of it."

Pete opened another bottle of Jack Daniel's, but only to lace the black coffee that his wife had brewed in an old tin pot on the stove. Maggie was given a blanket of patched skins and Schwarz was given a dose of penicillin.

"First thing you must know," Pete began, "is that skinwalker isn't an Eskimo term. It's an Indian word that the white man uses."

"But they do exist, don't they?" Maggie asked. "There really are people who can put on the skin of an animal, then take the animal's shape.

Pete smiled, another slow-breaking enigmatic smile. "Let me tell you something about Eskimo. You remember when those tough guys were out on the ice? You remember how they ran when I gave them my bear shout? They didn't see a bear. They didn't see anything, except a few little Eskimo in the fog. But as soon as they heard my bear shout, they turned tail and ran. Why? Because the bear shout made them imagine things. Well, the skinwalker is like that. Maybe it's just a guy who puts on a wolf's skin and then starts acting like a wolf. He doesn't really have to be a wolf in order to make people afraid."

"And why would someone want to do that?" Schwarz asked softly, meeting the old man's eyes and catching a glimpse of something he had not seen before—wisdom, strength. "Why would someone want to put on a wolf's skin?"

The old Eskimo smiled again, holding Schwarz's gaze for at least twenty seconds before shaking his head with a long and slow sigh. "Maybe so he can convince the Eskimo to give up his land."

Schwarz and Maggie exchanged another glance while the old man remained motionless. "I came here to stop them, Pete," Schwarz said as he leaned forward to meet the Eskimo's gaze again. "I came here to keep them from taking your land away. But in order to do that, I'm going to have to radio my associates and tell them to come out here."

The Eskimo pondered Schwarz's words for a long time before finally nodding. "You can radio your friends, but I don't think you'll be able to stop them from taking our land. I don't think anyone can stop them, because they're hungry. Besides, the old ways are gone. Nobody's interested in holding on to the land so they can hunt the whales or the seals. Today all they want is the money they get from letting the white men hunt for oil."

THE RADIO WAS KEPT at John Oovi's home. Like Pete's house, it was a cramped and ill-lighted place that smelled of boiled fat and burnt coffee. Upon entering the hut, the two Eskimo withdrew to the kitchen for a short exchange of whispered words. Schwarz was then told he could make one call, but only if he promised not to directly involve the village in his business.

"How are you going to do that?" Maggie asked when she and Schwarz were finally alone.

"How am I going to do what?" Schwarz replied, examining the radio, toying with the knobs.

"How are you going to keep these people from getting involved in whatever's going down here?"

Schwarz had found a scrap of paper and a pencil and had begun to work out a radio code. Looking up from his hasty calculations, he simply shook his head. "They're already involved," he said. "They were involved the moment they picked us off the ice and they know it."

"Then maybe we should warn them, explain to them what might happen."

Schwarz looked at her for a moment. Recalling the glint in the old Eskimo's eyes and the echo of that so-called bear shout on the ice, he simply shook his head again. "I think they know exactly what this game is all about."

The Able Team warrior switched on the power, adjusted the frequency and began speaking into the microphone. He spoke slowly and carefully, reading from the scrap of paper. Although fairly confident that Lyons and Blancanales would understand the message, he also knew that others would interpret it and that eventually they would converge on the little village.

18

By the time Sweeny and Denton received word of Schwarz's radio transmission, it was almost three o'clock in the afternoon and neither man had slept more than a couple of hours in the past twenty-four. Sweeny was feeling the effects of a cold, and Denton was trying to deal with a pounding headache.

"Why don't you just tell me where we stand?" Sweeny said, sucking on a throat lozenge in between sips of herbal tea.

Denton wiped his forehead with a handkerchief and continued staring out the window, watching a Caterpillar tractor move between the orange storage tanks. "It's still pretty sketchy," he said at last. "All we really know is that the girl and her bodyguard somehow managed to escape. Apparently they're hiding out in some remote native village about forty miles east of Barrow."

"And what about the other two? Lyons and Blancanales. Where the hell are they?"

Denton took a deep breath, his eyes now focused on the vast expanse of tundra beyond the tractor. "They're probably also at that village," he said. "Or at least not far away."

"And the village? What do we know about it?"

Denton shrugged. "Not much. It's just one of those little whaling villages. A dozen shacks on the shore, a couple of dozen drunken natives."

"Armed?"

"Not really. Probably just old Winchesters."

After another moment of silence, Sweeny placed his cup of tea on the table and smiled. "Well, in that case I think our problems are over."

He turned on the stereo and selected one of his favorite country tapes before retrieving a pad of paper and pen from the varnished oak desk. Then, finally seating himself on the red leather couch, Sweeny began to jot down his instructions.

"There's a guy out of Texas," he said. "Name is McNally. He's also got a partner in Denver. Name is Temple. I don't know what they charge these days, but give them whatever they want."

Denton stepped back to the window and pressed a hand to the thermal glass. "Don't you think that's going a little too far?" he said. "Our contract was to quash local resistance to the offshore program. It never called for—"

"Our contract calls for whatever measures are necessary to get the job done."

"And that includes murder?"

Sweeny laid down the fountain pen and rose to his feet. "Look, if we let this thing slide now, there's no telling what might happen. You understand me? I'm talking a grand jury investigation. I'm talking congressional inquiry. I'm talking big-time scandal. So you've got to stop asking yourself whether or not this thing is going too far, because the fact of the matter is that it's already too late. Things have gone way too far."

Another four or five seconds passed before Denton was able to tear himself away from the window. For a moment he looked very bad; his face was pale and his forehead was studded with perspiration. His voice, however, was steady when he finally managed to speak.

"What do I tell them to do about our magic Eskimo?" he asked.

Sweeny looked at him. "Huh?"

"Our shaman. Our wolf-man. If you're bringing in this outside talent, do you still want me to keep our wolf-man around?"

Sweeny thought for a moment, then shrugged. "Sure, why not? He's always good for a laugh and he scares the hell out of the natives."

TWO HOURS LATER, after ensuring that the line was relatively secure, Denton placed the telephone call to Thorton McNally in Plains, Texas.

"I'm calling on behalf of Mr. Crabb," Denton said, using a name that Sweeny had claimed would ring a bell.

"Oh, yeah," replied the sandpaper voice at the other end of the line. "And how is Mr. Crabb these days?"

"Mr. Crabb has a little public relations problem, sir."

"And exactly what kind of public relations problem would that be?"

"A three-man problem," Denton replied. "Three men and a young lady, to be exact."

There was a short pause, and Denton had the distinct impression that the speaker at the other end of the line was attempting to calculate the price of the hit.

"And where exactly are these three men and woman?" the man finally asked.

"North," Denton replied. "Far north."

"I hate the north," McNally replied.

"I understand that, but I think we can make it worth your while . . . financially speaking."

There was another pause, and Denton now had the impression that McNally was speaking to someone else.

"Let me ask you something," McNally said, coming back on the phone. "Why did Mr. Crabb ask you to call me?"

"Well, I think if you would—"

"Just answer the question, pal. Why did your Mr. Crabb ask you to call me?"

"Because the three men that are causing us a problem happen to be very able people. We need your expertise."

"Hmm," McNally breathed, and Denton was fairly certain that the man was smiling.

"So then can I assume that you will—"

"We'll be there tomorrow. But it's going to cost you a little more. In fact, it's going to cost you a lot more."

"How much more?"

"What difference does it make," McNally said, "as long as we handle the problem?"

The line went dead, and Denton replaced the receiver and then poured himself a stiff drink. He sank back down into a deep leather couch in front of the broad thermal window. For a while, comforted by the whiskey and the soothing view of the tundra, he was almost able to convince himself that everything would be all right, that very soon he could go back to the relatively normal existence he led as a public relations executive. But then, recalling his earlier conversation with Sweeny, he couldn't seem to keep his hands from shaking.

19

When old Pete had been a young man, he had believed that life was governed by spirits. Then the missionaries had come and the spirits had slowly retreated back out to the ice.

"But that doesn't mean that they don't have powers," the old Eskimo said. "It just means that you don't always feel them. But if you shoot a seal, and you don't give him a drink of water and sing a song to him, his spirit will take revenge on you. And that's something that the oilmen don't understand. You must treat the spirits right."

It was almost midnight. Lyons and Blancanales, who had appeared earlier, after decoding Schwarz's message, sat with the group on beanbag furniture and reindeer skins. As they listened to Pete, they ate a meal prepared by his wife.

"There's something your people have to realize," Lyons said, his gaze fixed on the old Eskimo. "The mere fact that we're sitting with you now may be enough to endanger this entire village and everyone in it."

Pete returned the warrior's gaze, and for a moment there were no sounds at all except for the gurgling pot of gray walrus blubber and the softer hiss of steam. Then finally he nodded. "As long as the white men walk our shores and scan the waters for oil, we are in danger. I think the spirits would be very offended if we failed to help you fight the oilmen who want to destroy our lands and the animals that live in our waters."

Another stocky Eskimo entered the hut, a young man with a dark and prematurely lined face. He was followed by an unusually tall boy, carrying an ancient carbine and an ivory knife. After whispering in old Pete's ear, the stocky young man withdrew to a corner of the room and began chewing on a dried slice of walrus meat.

"That man is called Irrigoo," Pete said. "His friend is Oovi, although everyone calls him Stringbean. They are the sons of my younger brother, Jack. Irrigoo has come to offer his help in our fight against the oilmen. He wants to kill the magic man who turns himself into a wolf."

Lyons looked at the men in the corner, studying the carbine for a moment and wondering how old it was. Twenty years? Thirty years? "I think those boys should understand something," he finally said. "It may not be just oilmen we're fighting. We may end up fighting professional killers, men who hunt other men with the same skill and determination that you people hunt the whales and seals. These killers may hire other killers who will come in helicopters. The body count could be quite high."

But the old man simply grinned again, his eyes fixed on the smoldering pot of walrus blubber and the clouds of drifting steam. "We understand," he finally breathed. "If they come to fight us on the ice, I don't think we have anything to worry about."

"SOMEBODY WANT TO GIVE me an assessment?" Lyons asked after the gathering had ended and the Able Team warriors managed to find themselves alone with Maggie. "Somebody want to tell me what the hell is going on here?"

Schwarz shrugged and turned his eyes to the far horizon. "I guess you might say it's like the old man told us," he said. "The spirits would be offended if they didn't help us."

"You've got to take their viewpoint on this," Maggie added. "These people are the old guard, the last of their kind. You put an oil rig offshore, and the sound of the drill alone will probably be enough to drive the whales away. You drive the whales away and these people are finished. Ten thousand years of culture and heritage—gone."

Blancanales stared at the ragged line of shacks behind them and the thin trails of smoke rising from the cramped linoleum kitchens. When they'd first arrived at the village, he had told Lyons he felt they'd stepped into a time warp. It was a feeling he couldn't shake, despite the snowmobiles and the satellite dish.

"I think there's something you're all forgetting," he said. "This isn't just a clear-cut environmental struggle anymore. This is war. That so-called public relations unit from the consortium is not going to let this slide, not after everything that's happened. They're going to have to throw everything they've got at us and more. They're going to have to try and end this problem right here and now, which probably means the employment of some very professional muscle. Now, you put these people against that kind of action, and you're going to see some real grief."

"So what are you suggesting, Pol?" Lyons asked.

Blancanales shook his head. "I'm not sure. I'm just saying that we don't have the right to involve these people."

"They're already involved," Maggie said. "They were involved the moment oil was discovered, and they're going to stay involved as long as they remain here. And you're not factoring in the most important issue."

"Which is?" Lyons asked.

"Even if *we* somehow managed to make our way out of here, these people will still be a target for the consortium. They know too much. They know who's behind the wolf murders, and they know why. And once they start spreading the word among other communities, the entire Eskimo population is going to reevaluate its stance on the offshore issue. That's something the consortium simply won't tolerate."

"So either way, they're doomed," Lyons said. "Is that what you're saying?"

Maggie shook her head. "Not necessarily."

"Then what?"

She looked at Schwarz and he nodded.

"There's something you've got to understand," Schwarz said. "Although these people may not look like much in the way of a fighting unit, they've got something that no one else has."

"You mean local knowledge," Blancanales suggested.

"It's more than that," Schwarz said. "It's—" He broke off, looking at Maggie again. "You tell them."

She took a deep breath, then fixed her eyes on the far horizon. "All I can tell you," she said at last, "is that the Eskimo culture is very old—ten, maybe fifteen thousand years at least. And although they may not have advanced in the material sense, they have definitely advanced in another sense. They definitely have certain powers."

"You mean the shaman stuff, right?" Blancanales said, not entirely able to suppress a smirk.

"She means power," Schwarz answered. "She means that these people have power."

Although Blancanales was still smirking, Lyons was dead serious when he spoke. "All right, then," the Able Team warrior began, "we'll stay. At least for the moment, we'll stay and fight."

20

"Tell me about the Eskimo," McNally demanded.

It was dawn and bitterly cold. Having flown all night on a chartered flight from Houston, McNally was exhausted. He was also angry, and whenever the big man was angry, he chewed on his handlebar mustache.

"So, what about the damn Eskimo?" McNally persisted as he surveyed his surroundings—the compound at Prudhoe Bay, the black stretch limo Denton had driven in to meet him and the storage tanks that were barely visible in the fog.

Denton shrugged, also scanning the lonely airstrip and the storage facilities. "There's not much to tell," he finally said. "They're just Eskimo."

"Do you want us take them out, too?"

Denton hesitated, returning his gaze to the twin-engine aircraft and the faces of McNally's team behind the frosted squares of Plexiglas. "Yeah," he finally said. "Take them all."

"Well, then, that's going to cost you extra," McNally said.

"How much extra?"

The big Texan shrugged. "Well, seeing how they're not likely to offer much resistance, I guess I can probably give you a little discount. Say, two hundred a head?"

Thorton McNally was a shadowy figure—even in the mercenary world. A three-tour veteran of the Central Intelligence Agency's infamous Phoenix Program in Vietnam, he was rumored to have collected more ears than any other white man in Southeast Asia. After the war, he moved around a lot: Guatemala, El Salvador, Angola and Zaire. Then, after taking nine shrapnel fragments in the legs and chest, he submerged for nearly a decade. When he finally surfaced again, it was as an undiscerning free-lancer. For a while he worked for the South Africans, hunting black nationalists for bounty. He then went to work for the Argentinians, the Colombians—anyone with hard cash and a need for a violent solution.

In addition to McNally, the little band of mercenaries included a half-mad explosives man named Jack Temple, two equally crazed brothers from Mississippi known as the Cosmo twins, and two neopunk killers who called themselves the Retro Rangers. The group represented everything that Sweeny had wanted and Denton had feared: They were a mindless force with no sense of right or wrong.

McNally had spent forty-five minutes waiting for Denton on the airstrip—forty-five minutes sitting in an icy Lear jet, staring through the frosted Plexiglas. He hadn't been sure who to go after first: the men Denton wanted dead, or Denton himself. He still wasn't sure.

"Well, then, we might as well get moving," Denton encouraged, interrupting McNally's thoughts.

"Sure," McNally replied. "Might as well."

Twenty minutes later, after stowing their weapons in the trunk, the six killers climbed into the limo. The driver, a stocky Oriental called Kulac, did not even glance at his passengers. He simply waited until Denton gave the word, then slowly pulled back onto the highway.

SWEENY WAITED in a darkened conference room adjacent to the executive lounge. Although caution dictated that he distance himself as much as possible from this operation, he had finally decided that he had an obligation to at least speak briefly with McNally. He wanted to explain and justify the mission.

Sweeny was still seated at the table when McNally finally entered the room. He jumped when the door slammed shut.

"So?" McNally said, his left hand rapping against his left thigh, the end of the handlebar mustache between his teeth.

"So how the hell are you?" Sweeny replied.

McNally shrugged, sank to a chair and reached for the decanter of cognac. "About the same."

Between them lay six feet of polished oak. On the paneled walls around them hung three landscapes of the west Texas plains and a portrait of Sam Houston.

"Quite a place you've got here," McNally said after slowly inspecting the room.

Sweeny offered the big man a thin smile. "We like it."

"But then you always had class, didn't you?" McNally added with an equally thin smile.

"I thought I'd give you a little background," Sweeny said at last. "Give you a little idea of what's at stake here, what it's really all about."

McNally shrugged. "If it makes you feel better, sure."

Sweeny rose from the conference table and moved to the map of the Arctic coast, hanging on the wall. "American's energy future," he said, sweeping his hand across the Beaufort sea. "Nobody knows exactly how much oil is out there, but we could be talking about as much as two-thirds of this nation's oil reserve. *Two thirds* and it's all just sitting out there waiting for us."

"Only the Eskimo won't let you dig—that your problem?"

Sweeny nodded. "Ever heard of the Alaska Native Claims Settlement Act? Rather than establishing reservations, a bunch of liberal congressmen decided to set up these native corporations to 'develop' the land. Now, a lot of these Eskimo know exactly which side of the bread has got the butter on it, and we get on with them just fine. But then you've got the group of old-liners, these 'Nanooks,' as we call 'em. Some guy in some little village who only wants to spear whales and pray to the spirits. Real pains in the ass."

"How many are you talking about?"

Sweeny shrugged. "It's not the numbers that matter. It's their influence. Some of these Nanooks have a lot of sway within their community. A lot of them are older. They've got seniority, and your average Eskimo respects that. So when these Nanooks start talking about how the offshore program is going to kill all the whales and anger the spirits, the others listen."

"Ever thought of playing their game? Giving them a little taste of the old psych-op program?"

"Oh, we've got that going. Hell, we've got the scariest damn Nanook monster you've ever seen, and it was starting to work out just fine, until about four days ago."

"Which is when their help appeared, that it?"

"Yeah," Sweeny breathed. "Carl Lyons and company."

McNally drew a quick breath at the mention of Carl Lyons, then rose from the conference table and moved to the map. His gaze, however, remained focused on the darkened view through the glass.

"You ever met Carl Lyons?" McNally asked.

"Yeah, I met him."

"Well, then you probably know that he's not just your average federal jerk. You go up against a guy like Lyons, and you have to be prepared to go the whole nine yards. You have to be prepared for the worst."

"There's only three of them," Sweeny put in.

"Yeah," McNally sighed. "Three of the meanest animals you'll ever meet. And let me tell you something about those men—they are incredibly adaptive. You put them out on the ice with a bunch of Eskimo whalers, and they'll find a way to fight you with spears if need be. And if they win, they'll drive it right on back here."

"Is this your way of saying that you want more money, or are you just trying to scare me?"

McNally turned from the darkened glass to face Sweeny with a tired smirk. "Neither. I just think you should realize the consequences. If my team fails to stop Carl Lyons and his boys, then they're going to be coming after you. Understand?"

21

The wind had risen, sweeping in another wave of ice fog. Now and again the silence of the empty landscape was broken by the sound of surfacing whales, but otherwise there were no signs of life, or at least none that Lyons could see. Yet from Pete's viewpoint, the tundra was virtually teeming with movement.

"Eskimo don't always stick together," the old man said to Lyons as they walked into the frigid twilight. "Sometimes they fight among themselves. Sometimes they don't even talk to one another. But right now they're all together. Right now they're whispering into their radios about these cannibals out at Prudhoe Bay."

"What do you mean?" Lyons asked.

The Eskimo tore off another piece of dried whale blubber and slowly began to chew. After a long moment's pause, he said, "That's what our people are calling them—cannibals."

"Did your people say how many of them there were?"

Old Pete held up a gloved hand. "About ten, but maybe only seven."

They continued walking, moving over the cold gravel to a rise above the shore. Below, two village girls were hefting plastic honey buckets into a pit, while two young boys tossed rubber spears at an abandoned Toyota four-wheel drive. Farther out along the slow-cracking floe, a squat figure appeared to be fishing through a hole in the ice.

"I can't bring your people into this," Lyons said at last. "I don't care about the arguments and the justifications. I just can't do it, not with the women and children in the village."

The old man merely shrugged. "While the men fight, the women and children will hide in the storage shed or in the kennels. They'll hide under the ground and they'll be safe because we'll draw the cannibals out onto the ice."

"And what if we can't keep them there?" Lyons asked. "What if we can't keep them out of the village?"

"Then we'll just have to rely on my magic songs."

Lyons was about to try to explain again exactly what it was like to face a fully automatic weapon, but the old man was clearly not interested in anything he had to say.

"Let me tell you a story," Pete said suddenly. "In the spring, when I was a boy, the white men came in whaling ships, working their way through the ice in search of our bowheads. At first we were happy to see them, because they brought Winchester rifles, hard bread and whiskey. But then we realized these white men were killing all the whales. They would kill the whale, cut out its jawbone and then leave the carcass to rot. Well, this was a bad thing. When the Eskimo kills a whale, he sings to the spirit and performs many sacred rituals to ensure that the spirit of the whale is not offended. He does this so the animals will continue to return. But this was not the way of the white man. The white man killed everything in his path until finally there were no more animals left, and many Eskimo died because they had nothing to eat."

The old man grew silent, watching the children and the hooded figure on the ice. "See that boy out there?" he asked softly. "That's how the Eskimo hunts. Silently, patiently. He uses spark plugs for sinkers and tomcod heads for bait, but he relies on his silence and patience. The white man does not understand. He hunts with big guns and machines and he frightens the animals away, and that's the end of the animals."

Lyons turned to watch the figure on the ice, saw him bait another line and then sink to his haunches to wait. "These killers, Pete, they're probably going to come in choppers," he finally said. "They're probably going to come fast and hard, and with fully automatic weapons. You understand what I'm saying? They'll come right down on top of us with fully automatic weapons."

But the old man only smiled. "Hey, you think I don't know about helicopters and machine guns? I know lots about that stuff. But I also know something else. I know that unless we fight, we're all going to die, anyway. So what damn difference does it make?"

PREPARATIONS BEGAN that night. Although historically the Eskimo have never waged a protracted war, they were by no means unfamiliar with the art of battle. In essence, old Pete told Lyons, the Eskimo had learned to hunt and fight according to the ways of the wolf. He moved quickly over the darkened tundra, driving his prey into a semicircle of death. He used the contours of the shore-fast ice to attack suddenly, and the blue-gray shadows of the ice heaves to withdraw unseen. Although he fought with a pack, he moved and killed as one.

"I think you will realize that the Eskimo fights with a great deal of courage," Pete told Lyons.

It was not quite midnight. Able Team had assembled in the relatively spacious house of a whaler named Elmer. Also present were Irrigoo and Oovi, the two younger whalers Lyons had seen earlier, and Maggie. Eventually, Pete had said, their force would number about seven or eight, because some of the villagers were still out with the whaling boats.

Lyons was not overly concerned with the numbers. He was worried about the women and children and the fact they would be virtually helpless if the killers decided to move in on the village. He also knew that his team would probably be facing advanced assault rifles with thirty-year-old carbines and a couple of deer rifles.

"I think we have to recognize the possibility that they may bring in something special for us," Lyons added. "Something fresh off the drawing board."

"But we also have something special," Pete countered. He turned to Oovi. "Show him the big bomb."

The stocky Eskimo stepped out to the passage, returning a moment later with what looked like a hand-stitched rifle case. It was a little over three feet long and decorated with tattoos of whales.

"Now, feast your eyes on this," old Pete grinned as the whaler withdrew what appeared to be a steel rod mounted atop an old harpoon.

"What the hell is it?" Blancanales asked.

"It's a darting gun," Maggie whispered. "It's what they use to hunt whales."

"That's right." Pete beamed. "And it's going to make quite an impression on those cannibals."

Lyons took the weapon and slowly turned it over in his hands. Originally designed in the early 1840s, the piece was essentially a gun-launched harpoon with a black-powder charge. It was adapted by the Eskimo in the late 1880s and represented one of the Eskimo's most enduring acceptances of white technology. Although it was quite effective against a forty or fifty-foot bowhead whale, Lyons didn't know how the weapon would be used against a man.

"The trick is to shorten the fuse," Oovi explained. "It becomes a type of grenade launcher."

But after examining the explosive mechanism, which essentially consisted of a crude percussion cap and a matchstick, Schwarz also showed his unease. "What happens if the plunger doesn't break the match?" he asked, demonstrating the action with his finger.

"Don't worry about that." Pete grinned. "These have been tested by experts." Then, suddenly letting the grin fade and lowering his voice to a whisper, he added, "Besides, this old thing isn't our secret weapon. It's much more powerful."

"Now what's he talking about?" Blancanales asked softly, sensing the strange tension around him, the almost frightened glances of Oovi and Irrigoo.

"He's talking about the songs," Maggie said. "He's referring to the shaman's songs."

Blancanales started to ask another question, but suddenly found himself silenced by a look in the old man's eyes.

"I know what you're thinking," Pete said. "You're thinking that I'm just one crazy Eskimo. But my songs have some pretty strong power to them. They have the power of the ice and the wind. They also have the power of the bear, which is more power than even a helicopter or one of those fancy new rifles has."

22

Thorton McNally had called a meeting of the members of his team in order to discuss the attack. They'd gathered in a floodlit warehouse about two miles southeast of the main compound at Prudhoe Bay. Although the interior of the warehouse had been ringed with space heaters, McNally's breath still fogged the air, and the waiting chopper had to be rigged with electrical heaters in order to keep the shafts from freezing. Regardless of the cold, however, McNally reassured his men there would be no problem with their weapons.

Specifically under discussion was the Steyr Advanced Assault Rifle. Representing the height of man-machine interface, the Steyr fired a 9.85-grain carbon steel dart at a muzzle velocity of over four thousand feet per second. The projectile, consisting of a synthetic-cased fléchette, rises only thirteen inches at midrange zeroed at six hundred yards. When ignited within the chamber, it will further produce almost sixty thousand pounds of pressure, allowing the weapon to release a 3-round salvo faster than imaginable. The Steyr also features a dual-magnification optical sight that allows the shooter to place the circle on the target and squeeze. There is virtually no recoil, and the accuracy is said to be almost supernatural.

After introducing the weapon to those of his men not familiar with it, McNally passed it to his left and into the hands of Jack Temple. Temple, after briefly hefting the weapon and examining its rounded bullpup design, passed it on to one of the Cosmo twins. Watching from the shadows behind the space heaters, Denton and Sweeny said nothing.

"In addition to these weapons, you may also elect to pack a handgun," McNally continued when the Steyr had been returned to him. "But frankly, gentlemen, I don't think you're going to need it. In fact, I don't think you're going to need anything beyond this baby."

"What will the enemy be packing?" the muscular Retro Ranger named Butch asked.

"As far as we know," McNally replied, "you're basically looking at deer rifles. Deer rifles and a few old carbines."

"What about the terrain?" a stocky Australian, who called himself Cookie, wondered.

"The terrain is pretty much what you've seen out here," McNally answered. "Ice and more ice."

Finally, stepping slowly out of the shadows, his rounded and pale form in stark contrast to his hired team of killers, Sweeny interrupted the session. "And how exactly do you plan to carry out this mission?"

McNally met his client's gaze and remained utterly silent for a moment. "We plan to find our targets and then shoot them," he responded before dismissing his men.

The men moved to the far end of the warehouse to relax. McNally did not follow them, but instead joined Sweeny and Denton in a tiny communications room adjacent to the building.

"You boys are running solo, aren't you?" McNally said after pouring himself a shot of brandy from Denton's silver flask. "You boys have gone out and hired my team, and the oil companies don't know a damn thing about it, do they?"

Sweeny also poured a shot of brandy into a coffee mug. "They don't have to know," he said. "They hired us to overcome local opposition to an offshore drilling program, and that's all we're doing. Period."

The muffled thumps of synthetic-cased fléchettes slamming into a pile of wet phone books back in the warehouse interrupted their conversation. The men were obviously testing the Steyr rifles.

"All I'm trying to tell you," McNally began again, "is that my boys can probably handle the hard end of this deal, but you're going to be left to cope with the rumors. You're still going to have to deal with a bunch of whispering natives and curious Feds. Now, I don't exactly know how the consortium operates, but I can't imagine that they're going to be real happy about the newspapers getting hold of this."

Sweeny took a long sip of brandy, then briefly shut his eyes as he swallowed it. "Public relations isn't your problem," he said. "Your problem is Able Team and whatever Nanooks they've managed to recruit."

McNally shrugged. "Hey, I'm just trying to tell you that this operation could get a little messy, and unless you people have some support upstairs..."

Sweeny simply shook his head. "Actually it's not the upstairs support that we care about. It's the downstairs support. It's what we have waiting in the basement that's probably going to make all the difference as far as the rumors are concerned."

McNally met Sweeny's gaze again, holding it as his eyes narrowed in suspicion. "What are you talking about?"

But Sweeny merely smiled and turned to Denton. "What do you say, Dent ol' boy? Shall we show him the beast now?"

Without waiting for an answer, the two men got up and left the room. McNally had no choice but to follow them. Beyond the communications shed lay a long concrete passage. It was heated, although McNally could not identify the source of that heat. He felt the throb of generators, but it was impossible to tell exactly where they were located. Then, as if from deep within the walls, he heard a guttural moan.

"I have to tell you," Sweeny said softly, "that when Denton first told me about this, I thought the boy had totally lost it."

At the end of the passage lay a narrow flight of steps that led to a green steel door. As they drew closer, it gradually became apparent that the guttural moan was actually a chant: dull and toneless, but with a definite form and rhythm.

"Now, I'm not saying that this character has supernatural powers," Sweeny continued, "but I will say that he's got one hell of a bag of tricks. The Eskimo are scared shitless of him, and that's what really counts...in a public relations sense, you understand."

Sweeny knocked twice on the door. Then, hearing a vague grunt from within, he slowly turned the handle as he cautioned his two companions, "Now, don't make any wisecracks, understand? These people won't understand no wisecracking Texas boys."

Initially McNally saw only shadows and then finally a slow-swaying form. Gradually, as someone lifted an oil lamp, he saw the outline of two figures seated on a heap of walrus skins: one of them a man, the other some sort of man-animal.

"Welcome to the world of primordial magic," Sweeny whispered. "Welcome to the Stone Age nightmare."

But as McNally stepped closer, peering into the creature's eyes, he began to realize that the nightmare was not quite as real as it seemed, that the wolf's head was rather poorly stitched in places, and patches of the fur were obviously synthetic.

"His name is Etok," Sweeny whispered, "and he's an Eskimo shaman. His friend calls himself Seevook, and he's Etok's assistant."

The two Eskimo regarded McNally with hostile glares, then exchanged a few whispered words. McNally, however, simply ignored them and turned to Sweeny again. "What is this shit?"

Sweeny smiled with a deferential nod to the seated Eskimo. "This here ain't shit, my friend. This here is what you call public relations. Now, obviously up close like this, Etok may not look like much. But if you were to see him out on the ice, howling and snarling, you would definitely believe that he was one bad wolf-man. Why? Because he believes it. You understand what I'm saying? You put that boy in a wolf's suit and you give him his set of wolf's teeth, and he *becomes* a wolf. I mean, he really *becomes* a wolf."

But, dropping to a squat so that his eyes were level with the Eskimo's eyes, McNally found himself looking at just another man—thirty, thirty-five years old, reasonably muscular, but ultimately just a man.

"So what's the deal?" McNally asked

Denton also stepped closer and squatted down by McNally's side. "The deal is that you're going to take Mr. Etok and his butler with you. You're going to take him out on the ice with you and let him do his stuff."

Ignoring Denton, McNally turned back to Sweeny. "You guys are kidding, right?"

"Not in the least." Sweeny smiled. "You see, you think Etok is just some Eskimo in a wolf's suit. But the Eskimo think he's a holy terror. Besides, it tends to confuse the issues, and that's exactly what we're trying to do with this offshore drilling program. Cloud the issues a little."

McNally started to protest, but was cut short by a sudden flurry of whispers from the shaman. When the shaman had grown silent again, the younger Eskimo finally spoke. "He wants to know who this man is and why he's here."

Sweeny glanced at McNally, then back to the younger Eskimo. "Tell him that this man is a soldier and that he's here to help us out on the ice. He's brought some friends with him, and they've got the sweetest-looking rifles you've ever seen."

After receiving the hushed translation, Etok seemed to ponder these words for a long time. He then turned to Seevook and grunted a quick reply.

"He says we don't need help out on the ice," the younger Eskimo replied. "He says that fancy rifles aren't going to make any difference, because now we're going to be fighting old Piitkaq and old Piitkaq has a song that is more powerful than any rifle. He also says that he doesn't like this soldier, that he's like a blind walrus that doesn't know that he's just bumped into a killer whale."

Sweeny cocked his head and frowned as if deeply concerned about the Eskimo's words. "Well, why don't you tell your boss that I understand his objections. However, I feel very confident about this gentleman, and I'd be deeply obliged if Etok would at least give the man a chance to prove himself."

Once again Seevook quickly translated Sweeny's words and waited for his response. "Etok says that he will give your soldiers a chance, but he warns you that old Piitkaq won't give anyone a chance. He says that once the old magic man starts singing his bear songs, nobody gets a chance. Nobody."

Although Sweeny and Denton nodded gravely, McNally couldn't keep himself from grinning. "Magic men? Bear songs? Tell me you guys are kidding."

23

"Who do we think we're kidding?" Blancanales asked softly.

He was seated on an old sofa in Oovi's home. A crucifix hung on the roughly-planked wall. The radio was tuned to a station in Nome that played hits from the fifties and sixties. An Eskimo woman named Doris was doing something in the kitchen with four-foot strips of bowhead blubber. On the wobbly card table lay virtually everything the village could muster in the way of arms and ammunition: six old carbines, a .22 Marlin rabbit rifle, a Remington Seven chambered for .308s, a couple of shotguns and a Mark VI Webley, circa 1915. There were also, of course, the whaling guns, but Blancanales was still not particularly impressed.

"Pol has a point," Lyons said, turning to Maggie. "Take away all the talk about magic songs and local knowledge, and basically we have nothing. We have an untrained force with a handful of popguns who are about to face some very hard professionals."

"But what's the alternative?" Maggie asked. "Even if we wanted to run, we couldn't possibly move everyone out of here. There simply aren't enough vehicles. Besides, these people won't leave their village. They'd rather die."

Schwarz appeared, followed by the lanky Eskimo who called himself Will. "We just received another radio signal," Schwarz said. "According to some of Pete's friends in Nuiqsut, a chopper is definitely on its way. Word has it, there's about a dozen of them, mostly white."

Lyons shook his head, then turned to Will. "How reliable are your friends in Nuiqsut?"

The whaler spread his lips to reveal a mouthful of yellowed teeth. "You mean could they mistake a goose for a big oil company helicopter?"

Before Lyons could reply, however, another whaler appeared, a strangely pale boy that everyone called Looki. After whispering in Will's ear, he announced that yet another shortwave radio transmission had been received, this one placing the chopper above Barrow.

Lyons digested the Eskimo's words then laid his hand on Maggie's shoulder. "We're going to try and keep the fight on the ice, but you've *got* to make sure that the women and children stay out of sight. You understand? They have got to stay out of sight."

The woman nodded, then turned her gaze to Blancanales.

But with his eyes still fixed on the heap of old weapons on the table, the Able Team warrior just shook his head again and whispered, "Who the hell do we think we're kidding?"

EACH SPRING, as warming currents swept northward, the shoreline became a battleground between the old ice and the new. Narrow channels widened into ponds, while broad packs cracked and swelled. The gravel beaches were left littered with frozen debris, and later, sink holes would open in the soggy ground. It was to such a place that old Pete led Able Team and his motley band of whalers—deep into the icy no-man's land where Eskimo have hunted since the beginning of time.

"Here's another story for you," Pete said as he and Lyons led the others out across the slow-breaking ice. "Once upon a time some Yankee sailors decided that they were going to steal the Eskimo ivory. They had also decided that they wanted a few of the Eskimo women to keep them warm at night. So they got out their rifles and they jumped off their ship, and they started marching to the village. But when they reached the village, they found that the Eskimo had hidden their ivory and taken their women out on the ice. One of the Yankee whalers who was knowledgeable about ice cautioned his captain against following them. He said that some of the ice was old and firm, but some was new and fragile. But the captain ordered his men to follow the Eskimo. No sooner had they stepped off the shore than the ice began to break and drift away. And that was the end of the Yankee sailors, who didn't know there was a difference between *genu*, which is old ice, and *sallek*, which is new ice.

Lyons glanced down to the ice at his feet, then out to the cracked plane of ice in front of him. "And which is this?" he asked. "Old or new?"

Old Pete smiled. "Good question."

They halted in the shadow of another frozen ridge amid tumbled blocks of ice. Now and again there was the distant crash of the cracking mantle as the warmer current collided with the cold, and long splinters of shore-fast ice slid into the sea. There was still no sign of the chopper.

"I think this is as good a place as any to fight them," old Pete said, sinking to his haunches at the base of the ridge.

Lyons also crouched into the shadow, but kept his gaze on the far north ground. Between the shifting rifts in the fog lay a shimmering band of black and gleaming-white pyramids of ice along the horizon. But the chopper, he told himself, would come from the south, hard and fast from the south.

"You've got to keep your people out of sight," he told the old man. "If they spot us from the air, we don't stand a chance. You've got to keep your people out of sight until the chopper lands."

The old man cocked his head. "Hey, you trying to tell Eskimo how to fight on the ice? That's like trying to tell a polar bear how to stay warm in the snow. Those cannibals in the chopper aren't going to see anything in this fog. They aren't going to see or hear anything until it's too late."

When the first strains of the chopper began cutting through the silence, Lyons could only think about what an automatic weapon could do to a man if it caught him in the open.

The chopper touched down half a mile south of the village on a flat stretch of tundra covered with grassy stubble. The cold was not as acute as McNally had anticipated, but the fog was much thicker. He was also concerned about the distant cloud banks he had seen at three thousand feet, and recalled stories he'd heard about the Arctic storms of early spring. But he wasn't worried about the mounds of jagged ice that ringed the frozen shore.

McNally moved out slowly, shielding his eyes from the wash of loose debris kicked up from rotating chopper blades. To his left were the bundled forms of the Retro Rangers, Butch and Cookie, their neopunk haircuts mercifully hidden beneath the hoods of their parkas. To his right were the slightly bulkier Cosmo brothers. Bringing up the rear was Jack Temple, looking vaguely like an alien in his silver thermal suit. The wolf-man and his handler, however, were apparently not ready to move.

They halted in a shallow patch of black moss about two hundred yards from the first of the village shacks. There were remnants of snowdrifts, clumps of bleached whale bones and walrus bones. There were also rusting barrels of human excrement, but no sign of human life.

"Maybe they split," the stocky Australian whispered.

"Yeah," Butch echoed. "Maybe they picked up our scent and split."

"Or maybe," one of the Cosmo twins whispered, "they're still in there . . . waiting."

A little closer to the village, they came across slices of whale blubber on a sawhorse. Then, without warning, they heard the first shotgun blast.

Jack Temple reacted first, spraying two quick salvos into the icy ridge along the shoreline. Butch followed with a second blind burst to the ridge, while Cookie sank to his knees with an enraged string of obscenities and three pellets in his shoulder and arm.

"All right," the blond Australian groaned, "that does it. That bloody does it."

McNally hurried over to the man and told him to lie still. Then, carefully prodding the punctured parka, he slowly examined the wound.

"That hurt?" he asked, his fingers pressing on the trace of seeping blood.

The Australian winced with a hard grin. "Of course it bloody hurts."

"You want to do anything about it?"

Cookie extended his arm, testing the joint and the muscles. Finally reaching for his Steyr again, he slowly rose to his feet. "Yeah, I want to do something about it. I want to bloody waste them."

For the moment they simply waited. Temple scanned the ice ridge through a pair of field glasses, the Cosmo twins scanned the far ground through the dual-magnification sights on their Steyrs and McNally attempted to pack Cookie's wounds with dressing. Finally, after Temple identified at least two vague shapes crouched along the ridge adjacent to the shoreline, they began to move out again.

They moved at a slow pace, away from the village and toward the water, keeping to the softer ground where clumps of Arctic grass offered a degree of shelter. Although McNally sensed that his team was growing increasingly tense, he also sensed a degree of relief—the enemy had identified its position, and now it was simply a question of closing the distance, moving into killing range and letting the Steyrs perform.

As they drew closer to the shore, it quickly crossed McNally's mind that the frozen terrain might pose a special hazard now that the spring thaw was under way. But just as quickly, he forgot the threat as the thrill of the hunt overcame him.

Old Pete had begun to sing—a soft, somewhat mumbled song.

"What's he saying?" Lyons asked softly.

He lay on his belly beside the stocky Oovi. When one of the younger whalers had panicked and let loose with the shotgun blast, both men had dropped to the shadows between two massive blocks of tide-shattered ice.

Oovi turned with a strangely passive gaze, his mittened hands still gripping his ancient carbine. "He sings about the bear," the whaler finally replied. "He sings about things that happened long ago but might happen again if our faith is strong."

"Our faith in what?" Lyons asked.

Oovi glanced up to the sky, then back to the fog-shrouded ice. "Our faith in the old ways."

There were sounds of boots on the ice behind them, then the gray form of Blancanales appeared, sliding down from the frozen blocks above.

"Far as I can tell, we're looking at about six or seven, with possibly another one or two still in the chopper," he whispered.

Lyons lifted his hand to shield his eyes from the foggy glare. "Any idea of their position?" he asked.

Blancanales nodded. "They're headed straight for us."

Schwarz appeared from the opposite end of the ice ridge where the nervous whaler had squeezed off the initial shotgun blast.

"We're definitely hit one," he said, "but I don't think it's even slowed them down."

"What about their weapons?" Lyons asked.

Schwarz shook his head. "Judging from the sound of the return fire, I think we're probably looking at something new, maybe one of the ARCs with a flé-chette mag."

"What about grenade launchers?"

"I didn't see anything like that, but then with an ARC you wouldn't need them out here, would you?"

Lyons took another look at the fog-shrouded landscape, then finally let the air hiss through his teeth. "All right," he sighed. "Pass the word to hold fire until my signal. You got it?"

Schwarz nodded. "I'll tell them, but I'm not sure they'll listen."

"Well, make them listen. We start trying to duke it out with ACRs, and we're going to be history within ten minutes. Our only hope is to keep them guessing, catch them from the angles and still keep them guessing."

"What about my people on the flank?" Blancanales asked, peering out to the dim forms of whalers crouched among the tumbled ice to his left.

"Same thing," Lyons replied. "They start firing early, and the game's over."

Schwarz and Blancanales moved out again at a half crouch. Moments after they had slipped back into the gray shadows, Oovi turned to Lyons. "Could be you have a good plan. Could be that you even know what you're doing. But somehow I don't think it's going to work for the traditional Eskimo."

"Yeah? And why not?" Lyons asked.

"Because traditional Eskimo don't fight that way. Traditional Eskimo fight according to what the spirits say. Then let the spirits dictate their actions.

Lyons was about to counter with a terse explanation of exactly what an ACR was and exactly what a 9.85-grain carbon steel dart could do to a human body. But before he could even open his mouth, his point was made for him when a 3-round salvo virtually decapitated one of the younger Eskimo.

The salvo had caught the younger man as he had risen to squeeze off another shotgun blast. It had caught him in the throat, and the 9.85-grain fléchettes traveling almost five thousand feet per second ultimately cut him in two, severed his spinal cord and pulverized the flesh and lower jaw so quickly that he didn't even have time to scream.

But Oovi screamed, a high scream of rage as he rose to his knees and squeezed off two blind rounds from his carbine. Before Lyons could drag him down again, three more fléchettes had pierced the fog.

"Stay down!" Lyons hissed. "You understand? Stay the hell down!"

There were four or five more sporadic shots, answered by another two salvos from the fog. Then, very briefly, Lyons finally caught a glimpse of his enemy: six ghostly figures, advancing very quickly through the ice on the tundra. And in their hands he saw the rounded polycarbonate stocks of the Steyr ACRs.

"We've got to pull back," he told Oovi. "You understand? We've got to pull back onto the ice."

The stocky Eskimo nodded, his eyes still locked on the mangled form of the body below.

Blancanales returned, scrambling up from behind the ridge. "We're never going to be able to hold them," he panted. "Not with what they're throwing at us now."

Lyons glanced to his left, where Irrigoo, Cosby, Elmer and Will were kneeling behind blocks of bullet-shattered ice. Somewhere deeper in the shadows, he knew Pete was also waiting. But apparently the autofire had not even broken his concentration.

"Where's Gadgets?" Lyons asked.

Blancanales pointed to a gray and indistinct form moving along the top of the ridge.

"All right," Lyons breathed. "This is how we play it. When Gadgets starts moving with the others out on to the ice, you and I are going to try to buy them a little time."

But even as Blancanales started to voice his objections, it was obvious that the shrouded figures weren't selling any more time....

Three more whistling salvos sent clouds of powdered ice rising from the ridge, and still another rain of fléchettes tore into the blocks of ice where the Eskimos crouched.

Someone, probably one of the younger Eskimo, let loose with a vintage revolver from the spine of the ridge, and Lyons didn't even have a chance to shout a warning before the ghostly figures replied with their Steyrs.

The Eskimo seemed to dance before he fell, an awkward little number across the ridge. Then, suddenly growing rigid as his parka exploded in blood, he tumbled like a rag doll into the shadows.

It seemed that the air was then alive with whistling fléchettes. Lyons and Blancanales managed to squeeze off a couple of futile rounds, but then simply found themselves hugging the ground, their faces down, lips pressed to the ice.

When the shooting finally abated and Lyons was able to safely take another look, he caught another glimpse of the enemy moving in from the tundra. But given the power and range of the Steyrs, he and Blancanales simply started retreating.

They moved in a low crouch, keeping to the shadows of the ice mounds. As they passed beyond the shoreline and out onto the ice, they heard another 3-round salvo screaming in answer to a few random shots. But at the same time, they also heard the tuneless echo of old Pete's song....

Finally there was only a deep and cold silence as the frozen mantle continued to sway on the oily sea.

McNally drew his men to a halt and scanned the mantle of ice beyond the shoreline. Although there was clearly some sort of movement in the shadows of the frozen ridges, he wasn't sure if it was human. Nor was he sure of the source of the singing he was certain he'd heard.

"You got a problem?" Temple asked, his rangy body crouched and tense.

McNally lifted his field glasses and focused on what might have been some sort of walrus peering from between two swaying blocks of ice. "I don't know," he finally breathed. "Maybe something's not right."

Cookie, the neopunk Australian, slid up behind the wedge of ice beside McNally. "We definitely got ourselves two of 'em," he drawled. "Two Nanooks ready for mounting."

McNally shifted his gaze to what might have been a party of polar bears moving through the fog. Finally laying the glasses down again, he turned to the Australian and told him to bring the others up. "And tell them to keep low," he added. "Tell them to keep low and keep quiet."

When the Australian had slipped away, McNally once more began to scan the ice, following the tracks of the fissures to a vanishing point in the fog.

"So?" Temple asked after another three or four minutes of silence.

But once again McNally simply shook his head and sighed. "I don't know. Something's just not right. It just doesn't feel right."

"Which means what? You want to get the chopper? See if we can nail them from the air?"

McNally glanced up at the sky, at the swirling mist rolling in from the sea. "No, the chopper wouldn't do us any good, not with the fog."

"Then how about getting those Eskimo? That shaman character and his buddy, how about we get those two out here to cut us a trail?"

McNally again shook his head. "No, this is something we're going to have to do ourselves."

But when the bulk of his team finally appeared McNally still didn't seem entirely certain that he wanted to take the battle out onto the ice.

As a result, he led his men out slowly. In an effort to gain some perspective on the battlefield, he thought briefly of other places he had fought: the rice paddies of Southeast Asia, the jungles of Central America, the plains of North Africa. In the end, however, he knew that he had never seen anything quite like the frozen mantle of the Beaufort Sea.

He cocked his arm, drawing his team to a halt behind another mound of ice. Ahead lay a landscape that seemed no less forboding than the face of some distant planet, a place of deep secrets and chilling revelations. Below lay water colder than any mind could imagine.

"What do you think?" Temple asked softly, crouching beside McNally in the vaguely blue shadows of the fifteen-foot heave. All around them lay mounds of bluish ice thrown up by the pressure of the thaw.

"I think," McNally replied softly, "that we've probably reached the end of the line."

They started out again at a slightly quicker pace, driven by the cold. At fifty yards one of the Cosmo twins claimed he saw something moving between the jagged mounds of ice sixty yards to the north. As they drew closer, they saw nothing but the wisps of fog.

"Let me ask you something," the Australian said as they slipped between two almost perfectly triangular blocks of ice that might have been sculpted by some ancient hand. "You think there's anything to all that shaman mumbo jumbo?"

McNally shrugged but didn't stop scanning the white forms of tumbled ice ahead. "What difference does it make?"

Cookie shook his head. "I don't know. I was just thinking."

"And what?"

"About that wolf-man in the chopper, about what he kept saying about that old Pete character."

"Yeah, well I wouldn't worry about it."

"I'm not saying I'm worried. I'm just wondering if there's anything to it. I'm just wondering if maybe we shouldn't have taken some precautions."

McNally looked at the lanky killer from the Australian outback and smirked. "What kind of precautions, mate? You think maybe we should have rubbed ourselves in whale grease? That what you're talking about? Look, I don't need that kind of shit right now. You understand? I don't need that—"

He broke off suddenly, growing stiff and silent as another tuneless song came wafting out of the fog.

"What the hell is that?" one of the Cosmo twins whispered.

They drew to a stop in a circular crater. Although none of McNally's men had said anything, the tension had suddenly grown thicker, descending heavily around them. There was also a sense of movement beneath their feet, as if a herd of bowhead whales had begun softly nudging the underside of the ice.

But most disturbing of all was the song: low and mournful.

"It's nothing," McNally whispered to his huddled team around him. "You boys understand? It's nothing."

But by now the deeper notes seemed to reverberate directly through the ice, setting up a deadly vibration that widened the tiny cracks into fissures, the fissures into gaping channels.

Then, without warning, an entire section of the mantle began to crumble, slipping into the churning water with a hiss of icy spray.

"I think we'd better get out of here," Temple whispered.

"It's breaking up!" someone else yelled.

Yet all McNally finally heard were the shots—three distant cracks of a deer rifle from somewhere deep within the fog. And then he saw the face of the Australian Retro Ranger, the lean pale face suddenly explode in blood and a cloud of stuffing from his parka.

"Let's go!" he shouted, scrambling back across the cracking ice. "Let's go!"

There were two more shots from the swirling fog, and one of the Cosmo twins skidded to his knees with a bullet in the elbow. "Shit!" the boy screamed, rolling on his side as the blood spurted onto the glossy white mantle and a second bullet tore off an inch of flesh at his shoulder.

McNally watched the twin thrash as the ice began crumbling under him, the crack widening to a gaping fissure as the sea rose up to consume him. He heard a second terrified scream, then caught another glimpse of the boy frantically struggling for a handhold on the steep wedge of bobbing ice.

As the vibrating moan of the unearthly song continued booming out of the fog and the ice continued crumbling, the boy slid out of sight. Although he briefly reappeared, rocketing up with the shock of the cold sea, just as suddenly he was gone again, sinking into the blackness below the icy mantle.

"Let's go," McNally said softly. He spoke louder when no one responded. "Let's go. Right now, let's go!"

Finally, as if roused from a bad dream, the remaining band of mercenaries slowly started picking their way back through the icy rubble. When they reached the cold gravel along the shore, they dropped to their bellies to scan the frozen sea. Apart from the occasional crack of the mantle, however, it was once more silent.

27

Lyons laid down his deer rifle and looked out across the silent landscape. Although the old man had finally stopped singing, Lyons was still haunted by the sound; he still felt it in the pit of his stomach.

"Any sign of them?" Blancanales asked, slipping into the shallow crater of ice where Lyons lay.

Lyons picked up the field glasses and scanned the long expanse of cracked ice. "No, nothing."

"But you're pretty sure that you took down at least two of them, right?"

Lyons laid down the glasses. "No," he said. "I only took down one. Pete took out the other man."

One of the younger Eskimo appeared, slipping into the crater quietly. "Pete says that the ice is safe again," the boy said. "He says that if you want to chase them back to Prudhoe Bay, go right ahead because the ice will hold you now."

Lyons glanced over his shoulder to the slow-swaying outline of the old man on an icy mound. "I think it's time I had a talk with Pete," the Able Team warrior responded as he got up from the ice.

But when Lyons reached the old Eskimo, Pete simply continued staring out to the gray wastes.

"I know what you're thinking," he said at last. "You're wondering if what you saw was real or not.

You're wondering if it was my song that made the ice crack, or if it was something that just happened."

Lyons crouched down on the ice, his deer rifle across his knees. "You're right," he finally replied. "I'm wondering if what I saw was real."

The old man smiled and tapped a mittened finger to his forehead. "That's the problem with white men," he said. "They think too much. They see something that they don't understand and they try to make sense of it. The Eskimo doesn't do that. The Eskimo accepts that there are certain things that he will never understand, and he lets it go at that."

"And what happens when those things start killing people? What does the Eskimo do then?" Lyons asked.

The old man leveled his coal-black gaze directly into Lyons's eyes. "Then he calls upon someone like me, someone who knows the ancient songs."

The old man rose to his feet and turned to face the shoreline again. "I can't tell the future. I can't look into a hole in the ice and tell you what's going to happen tomorrow or what's going to happen in a week's time. But I can tell you this much. Before the day is over, you will need my power to help you fight what's out there. Even though you have a good eye and a steady hand with that rifle, sooner or later you're going to need me. You're going to face something that your rifle won't stop, and when that happens, you're going to realize the power the old magic songs possess."

Lyons also rose to his feet, shifting his gaze to the long view of icy mantle and the fog-obscured tundra beyond. Although there were several things he might have said in response, several perfectly rational and scientific arguments he might have used to counter the old man's words, he said nothing. He simply stood there, gazing out to the mist-shrouded shore where the next phase of the battle would be fought.

28

McNally picked up his weapon and jammed in a fresh magazine of fléchettes. Moments earlier Butch had suddenly flown into a seething rage, shouting that he was sick and tired of just sitting around while the bodies of his buddies were turned into ice cubes. McNally had had to slap the kid across the face in order to shut him up.

He knew now was the time to speak to his men. "All right, I've taken enough of your crap," he said as he rose to his feet. "Now, I want everyone to be quiet and listen up. We took a little bruising out there, but that doesn't mean we have to start going crazy. It just means that we have to change our tactics, that we have to hit from another angle."

Temple, too, rose to his feet. "Don't get me wrong," he said, "but something tells me that the angles aren't going to make a whole lot of difference out here."

"Yeah?" McNally countered. "Well, let's see how they like it when we start taking their village apart."

"What are you talking about?" the remaining Cosmo twin asked, his eyes narrowed to slits.

McNally nodded toward the faint outline of the huts looming in the fog. "I'm talking about moving onto the village and seeing if there's anyone hiding out there," he answered. "I'm talking about giving their little Eskimo broods a taste of the Steyr. Now, how do you boys feel about that?"

Temple smiled, then also jammed a fresh magazine into his weapon. "I think we feel fine about it," he said as McNally began to regroup the team.

IT WAS ABOUT four hundred yards to the first lonely shacks of the village, four hundred hard yards across a stretch of frozen tundra. Although none of his men actually said anything, McNally sensed their growing rage with each slow step. Two of their buddies had been eaten by the ice, and now the survivors were mad. It was in their eyes and in the way they gripped their weapons, the way they kept working their jaws. What had begun as just another job was becoming a vendetta.

McNally also sensed their uneasiness, a deep and irrational uneasiness about what lay waiting in the fog.

"Let me ask you something," Butch said as he sidled a little closer to McNally without breaking his pace. "What do you think that thing was out there?"

McNally gave the stocky boy a sidelong glance. "What thing?"

The neopunk killer cocked his head to the shore-fast ice. "You know. That thing that was moaning out there. The thing that made Cook lose it."

McNally hesitated, recalling the unreal sound they'd heard as the ice began to crumble. Then he suddenly shook his head with a frown. "I think it was bullshit."

They halted as they drew in sight of the village, kneeling in a patch of black lichen and Arctic grass. Although there were still no obvious signs of life among the shacks, there was definitely a *sense* of someone out there... waiting, watching, terrified.

"Now, listen up," McNally said as he hefted his weapon and dropped the safety. "I realize that you boys are a little pissed off right now, but I want some hostages out of this one. You understand what I'm saying? Assuming there are still people in that village, I want some hostages."

"I hear tell that some of them Eskimo women can get pretty mean when you try and rope 'em," the surviving Cosmo twin said with a slow and tuneless drawl.

"I want some hostages," McNally repeated.

They started out again at a slower pace, moving in a ragged line across the ground. At a hundred yards McNally was fairly certain that he saw something slip between the shadows of a shack. Then at fifty yards he heard the dogs.

It's just like Nam, he told himself. While papa and big brother hit you from the flanks, momma and kids stay home and booby-trap the village. Only here, he thought with a faint smile, there was no jungle, which meant that there was no place to run and no place to hide.

He drew his men to a halt again in a shallow depression forty yards from the first dark shack. Although the village was still quiet, he was sure he'd heard a noise from within the first shack. There was also something moving between the dung pits, running for shelter in one of the rear shacks.

Hey, Carl Lyons, McNally thought grimly. You came here to protect these people, and now I'm about to eat them alive.

"Remember, I want hostages," he repeated one more time.

They took the last forty yards at a half run, their weapons sweeping the ground in front of them, their gazes fixed behind plastic goggles. At twenty yards the Cosmo twin squeezed off the first salvo at what appeared to be a frightened face in the window but turned out to be his imagination.

Then he saw the dogs.

The dogs had been crouching between the first and second shacks, seven classic huskies trained to the sled. At the sound of the rushing men, however, they had suddenly grown agitated, yelping in fear.

And then Butch opened up with his Steyr.

He caught the first dog as it tried to run through a doorway, rump-shot him so that the animal lost the use of its hind legs, then shot it again as it attempted to drag itself to safety. He caught the second and the third dogs as the animals tore off toward the shore, dropped them in their tracks with a burst to their bellies. Then, as four more animals turned to fight, snarling with every last ounce of instinctual rage, Temple and the Cosmo twin also opened up, spraying blood, flesh and bits of fur at least ten feet into the air.

There was another muffled cry from somewhere deep within the cluster of shacks, and for a moment McNally thought that one of the dogs must have managed to drag itself off to shelter. He imagined the wounded animal shivering in pain on the cold ground, its legs blown to stumps by the steel darts. But then something about the way the cry was silenced as if by a human hand made him think again.

And while still considering the possibility that maybe, just maybe Lyons and his team had screwed up bad, he heard the cry again. It was definitely human.

"You hear that?" he asked softly.

Butch and the Cosmo twin nodded while Temple said, "Yeah. We heard it."

Maggie pressed her hand to the child's mouth once again and met the frightened glances of the others. It was cold in the storage shed and still colder beneath the old plank floorboards. There were also unpleasant odors: a stench of frozen blubber, ancient urine and whale flesh. In all, there were sixteen women and children hiding in the shed. At the opposite end of the village, crouched beneath planks of rotting pine, were the remainder of the community's frightened population—another eight women and children. They waited in a shallow hole that had been scraped out of the permafrost, waited just as their ancestors had waited while their men had been off fighting Yankee whalers on the ice.

I should have convinced these people to leave, Maggie told herself. I should have convinced them to pile into the trucks and drive away. But she knew that her plea would have been ignored. An Eskimo woman would never abandon her home, not while her man was still out on the ice.

Maggie heard footsteps now, the slow tread of a man's boot just outside the door of the planked shed. She felt the child stir in her arms again.

"Don't cry, baby. Don't cry," she whispered soothingly. She heard another soft footstep on the hard ground, then met the eyes of an Eskimo woman named Helen as they recognized the click-click of a cocking weapon. A woman called Tookie eased back the hammers on an old twelve-gauge. Then for a moment Maggie heard and saw nothing...as she shut her eyes and repeated the only prayer she knew.

"WANT TO KNOW a secret?" the Cosmo twin whispered to McNally.

McNally took another step closer to the boy's side. They had reached the end of the first row of shacks and now stood by a weathered structure that was probably an outhouse. The roof was made of corrugated iron, and the walls had been fashioned with planks of uneven timber. And although there were no immediate signs of life in the shack, there was definitely a well-trodden path leading to it.

"You hear them?" McNally asked softly.

The boy shook his head, then tapped a finger to his nose. "I don't hear 'em." he grinned. "But think I smell 'em."

Temple approached, moving on the balls of his feet and choosing his steps very carefully. "There's some sort of little hovel at the end of the road," he said. "Looks like somebody might be hiding underneath it."

McNally nodded, then extended a hand to the doorway of what was really the storage shed. "Same here," he whispered.

"Then how about I go in there and flush 'em out?" the twin whispered. "Huh? What do you say?"

McNally hesitated, once more recalling the echo and the vision of his man thrashing in the dead cold. "No,

I think we can do it from here," he finally said, leveling the muzzle of his Steyr at the doorway.

MAGGIE PRAYED for a miracle. She prayed that something would intervene and prevent their certain massacre.

And then, as if her prayers had been heard, the wind began to rise again, churning like a tiny gale and sweeping in from across the ice. She heard shouts as the gravel began to rattle against the planked siding and the chilled air clawed at the corrugated roofing. And all around her, the eyes of the Eskimo women had begun to shine as their lips mouthed a prayer to the Spirit of the Ice.

MCNALLY DROPPED to his knees and pressed his hands against his eyes. Beside him Temple had begun shouting something about the Steyr, but his words were lost in the roar of the wind and the rattle of gravel. The Cosmo twin began to shout, but his voice was also ripped to shreds by the wind.

Something slammed into McNally's shoulder, and he realized that the swirling gravel had peppered his face with tiny cuts. He couldn't find his weapon, and he searched the area, his eyes finally resting on the Cosmo twin, who had curled into a fetal position.

Someone, probably Butch, began to shout. "What the hell is going on?" he yelled.

But it wasn't until McNally heard that low and menacing chant again that he finally understood.

"Don't try to figure it out," Lyons said. "Don't even think about it. Let's just move out."

From where he and his team now crouched, they had only been able to vaguely follow what had happened. The killers had peered into the storage shed where Maggie and the other women were huddled; their Steyrs had been leveled at the floorboards and were obviously ready to fire. Then very suddenly, as old Pete began to chant... the wind developed the fierceness of a hurricane.

"Move!" Blancanales shouted to the Eskimo behind him. "Let's go! Move out!"

Yet even as the bundled figures rose, breaking into an awkward run, the strangely ominous chant continued. Just as the wind continued clawing at the killers.

"We've got to scatter them!" Schwarz screamed. "Once they get their bearings again, they're going to open up on the people in that shed."

Realizing that the flurry of the wind had only bought them a few precious seconds, Lyons had already drawn his .45 auto. Not that he had a chance in hell of hitting anything at two hundred yards, but at least he could keep the killers occupied. He could distract them from slaughtering the women and children.

The Able Team warrior squeezed off four shots on the run, four quick shots to let them know he was coming. From over his left shoulder, Blancanales also began squeezing off shots, while Schwarz let loose with his deer rifle....

But it wasn't until old Elmer let loose with his explosive whaling harpoon that McNally's team was obviously under attack.

McNALLY WAS STILL on his knees when the black-powder bomb from the harpoon gun exploded. Although it did not possess the power of a modern grenade launcher, the eight-gauge device was generally more than sufficient to kill a whale—and powerful enough to do ugly things to the Cosmo twin.

Once again McNally only saw the hit from the corner of his eye. One moment the stocky twin was rising to his knees, shouting as he swung his Steyr toward the rushing Eskimo. The next moment his entire torso seemed to disintegrate in a cloud of blood and fragmented flesh as the three-foot harpoon pierced his chest and exploded.

Butch and Temple both screamed at the sight of their friend's mutilated body.

"Let's get out of here!" McNally shouted. "Now! Right now!"

A second black-powder harpoon exploded to McNally's left, sending fragments of roofing material raining down on the squatting mercenary. He caught a glimpse of Butch and Temple scrambling for cover behind one of the shacks. When he turned, he found himself the target of an Eskimo who was leveling an old carbine. McNally went into a roll as the first slug kicked up a tiny cloud of dark earth and then he scrambled for shelter as four more heavy slugs pounded into the ground around him.

"We just got to let them get in closer," he told Temple.

But Temple could think only of the weapon that had destroyed the Cosmo twin. "What the hell was that thing? What the hell was it?"

"They're circling around," Butch interrupted from his vantage point at the corner of the shed. "They're circling around to make sure we don't hit their women."

But McNally merely smirked. "Forget the women. I want that bastard that did the twin. And I want Lyons."

Four more slugs slammed into the walls of the shack. There was an echo of shattering porcelain and glass, then the high yelp of another wounded dog. McNally responded with three fast salvos sprayed out from one corner of the building, while Temple followed suit from the opposite end of the shack. But it wasn't until Butch had reached the roof that the full effect of the Steyr became obvious again.

The roof gently sloped away from a makeshift chimney, and the tar tended to give under Butch's weight. But his line of fire was initially so perfect that he couldn't keep from talking to himself. "Want some?" he whispered. Then, aligning the sight with a stocky Eskimo between a row of sheds, he yelled, "Come and get it, come and get some!"

The first three steel darts caught the Eskimo in the shoulder, tore off an enormous hunk of flesh and bone and threw him against a door. The next three projectiles struck his stomach, sending long strings of intestines spewing into the air.

He caught the second Eskimo as he attempted to scramble behind a Toyota truck, caught him in the legs and actually saw the booted foot explode into the air. Then, finally catching a glimpse of the man he knew to be Carl Lyons, he squeezed off another salvo.

But Lyons had dropped into a roll and was already on his feet again, swinging out from behind a bullet-riddled shed, bringing up what looked like an ancient harpoon. And as Lyons let the weapon fly, Butch suddenly realized it was a whaler's gun.

The four-foot harpoon caught him just above the groin, yet for a moment there was nothing—merely the kick of the thing and the shock of steel inside his body. Just as he managed to scream, the hammer sent the firing pin into the primer and he actually felt his body explode.

Temple finished the boy's scream, throwing back his head with a trailing, *Noooooo!* And he would have continued screaming if McNally hadn't grabbed his arm and yanked him to his feet.

"Let's go. Come on, let's go!"

There was a dull reverberation from another whaling bomb, which exploded, sending a shower of splinters. But once McNally and Temple had managed to scramble past the last shack and into a shallow ravine beyond the village, it was suddenly very quiet again.

"That does it," Temple said, breaking the silence.

They had come to a stop about fifty yards beyond the last shack. Although there were still random shots ringing out from within the village, McNally knew he had to calm Temple.

"Butch is dead," he said. "You understand? That's the first thing you've got to come to terms with. Butch is dead and nothing's going to change that. Cookie's also dead, as are the Cosmo twins. It's just you and me now. I underestimated these people. I thought we were going in for a duck shoot, and it turned out that the ducks had the best weapons. So if we're going to make it out of here, we've got to find some way to even the score."

Temple rolled on his side, peering over the edge of the gravel ridge toward the empty row of Eskimo shacks. Although a terrified dog continued to yelp, there were no other sounds at all, not even the wind.

"All right," Temple finally breathed. "What have you got in mind?"

"I'm not sure exactly, but I do know this much—there's some strange shit going on out there and I think it's about time that we got our hands on a little of it."

Temple glanced over his shoulder to the empty stretch of tundra and the wall of ice fog. "Look, if you're thinking about bringing in that wolf-man, then you'd better have your head examined."

"All I'm thinking," McNally replied, "is that these people are into some strange shit and it's destroying us. Now, I don't necessarily believe in any so-called special powers, but I do know that sometimes you've got to stretch the parameters a little. So let's just get the hell back to the chopper and tell that wolf-man to do his thing."

31

An elderly Eskimo produced an old telescope from deep within her parka. After three or four minutes of scanning the mist-layered landscape, she simply shook her head and claimed, "They're gone. They took one look at my boys and they turned their tail and ran away never to come back."

Lyons wasn't so sure that his enemy wouldn't be back. He laid down his deer rifle and left the group surrounding the woman to confer with Blancanales. Pol was examining the body of the fallen Retro Ranger. "Anything?" Lyons asked.

Blancanales drew the fallen mercenary's hood over the pale features and shook his head. "No, these guys are way too professional to carry anything in their pockets. They're too professional to do anything but die."

After emerging with the women and children from the storage shed, Maggie had also spent a moment or two examining the bodies of the dead. Although she was apparently under control, Lyons noted that her cheeks were already tracked with tears.

"It's almost over," he told her. "One way or another, it's almost over."

Maggie simply shook her head. "It's never going to be over. As long as these people try to hold on to a land that the white man wants, it's not going to end. They're going to have to keep on fighting and dying."

He laid a hand on her shoulder. "Maggie, I have to ask you about that wind, about what happened when the old man started chanting."

She turned and looked at him with a faintly bitter smirk. "If you have to ask, you'll never understand."

He let his hand slip from her shoulder but didn't let go of her gaze. "That's not an answer and you know it."

"All right, then try this one on for size. Pete is a shaman—the real thing. His songs are incantations, and they're as old as the ice beneath your feet. Five, ten, at least fifteen thousand years. And although nobody really understands it, somehow he managed to tap into some very elemental powers—the wind, the cold, the pressures under the ice. Somehow he's managed to get it all under his control."

"And you believe that?"

She gave him a weary shrug. "I believe what I saw, what I heard."

He left her standing between the rows of shacks, some with blown windows, others with bullet-riddled walls. Lyons left her without a word and continued moving toward the gravel ridge where Schwarz and Blancanales were waiting with the whalers. As Lyons drew closer to the cluster of Eskimo, however, there were no sounds beyond old Pete's voice. Although the Eskimo spoke in his native tongue and so softly that it was hardly more than a whisper, the tone was unmistakable—the tone of death and sorrow.

"Pete says that the worst is yet to come," Irrigoo said as Lyons entered the circle around the old man. "He says that more of us are going to suffer before the day is over. But he says his magic is still strong and that we shouldn't be afraid."

Lyons moved to the old man's side and squatted on the gravel. "I want you to tell your people to leave the village. Tell them to go out on the ice or up the coast, but tell them to get out of here."

Old Pete turned to meet Lyons's imploring gaze. "If we leave, you and your friends will die. Even though you're superior warriors, you will die when the bad thing returns."

Schwarz stepped forward, whispering into Lyons's ear. "He's talking about the wolf-man," he said. "That's what all this is about. They're convinced that the wolf-man is going to return."

Lyons returned his face to the impassive profile of the old Eskimo beside him. "Is that true, Pete?" he asked. "Is that what you think is going to happen? You think the guy in the wolf suit is coming back?"

Old Pete shook his head. "He's not just a guy, Carl Lyons. He's a shaman, and when he puts on that suit he *is* the wolf. He is the wolf of the tundra and the wolf of the mountains. But he's also the wolf of the spirits, which is why you can't shoot him or harpoon him. The only way you can kill him is with stronger magic. With the magic of my spirit—bear."

Lyons ran a hand across his mouth, glanced at Schwarz and Blancanales, then back to the old Eskimo. "How about we play it like this? You take your people out on the ice and sing your songs. Meanwhile we will—"

"You and your men will die. If I'm not here to fight with you, you and your men will die. It's too late to run to the ice. The wolf is already closing fast. He will come out of the fog, and our only chance now is to fight him."

Lyons picked up his rifle and removed a fresh box of cartridges from the deep pockets of his parka. "Okay," he said loudly enough for all those around to hear, "if that's the way your people want it, then we'll stay here and fight. We'll stay here and fight together."

Old Pete placed a leathery hand on Lyons's shoulder. "Yes, we can fight together," he said. "But we're not going to kill that wolf with a rifle. The only way we're going to kill him is with more magic."

No one dared to contradict old Pete as an unmistakable howl rolled in from the fog.

"I don't believe this," Temple whispered.

They were crouched in the door of the chopper, their weapons across their knees, a flask between them. The pilot was reading a paperback novel as the radio played country music.

And not more than forty feet away, squatting on his haunches, the shaman known as Etok was becoming more wolflike.

The Eskimo had first laid the wolf's skin over his shoulders while Seevook chanted softly in the background. Then, with slow and precise movements, he had somehow managed to slip *inside* the skin . . . to actually draw it over his naked body as if merging with it. Then he had begun to sing, softly and hypnotically. Finally, rocking back and forth on his haunches, he began to sniff the air.

"He's ready now," Seevook finally told McNally. "He's ready to work his ways."

McNally nodded and rose to his feet. "All right, then let's move out."

They proceeded toward the village at a moderate jog, McNally and Temple about thirty feet behind the shaman and his apprentice. Although the shaman walked on two legs, there was definitely something very lupine to his gait and to the way he would pause to sniff the air.

They drew to a halt along another patch of Arctic grassland two or three hundred yards from the village. Although the shacks were still obscured by the fog, Etok obviously sensed the proximity of the villagers. He swayed on his haunches again, head cocked, nose in the air as a strange guttural moan issued from his throat.

"What the hell is he doing now?" Temple asked. "You want to tell me what the hell he thinks he's doing?"

McNally finally told him only to shut up.

Seevook approached, leaving his master still swaying on his haunches and fingering some sort of clawed weapon that obviously duplicated the ripping fangs of a real wolf.

"Etok says you should wait here," the boy said to McNally. "He also says that you shouldn't be scared if you start hearing bad things."

"Who's this guy trying to kid, huh?" Temple whispered to McNally.

Ignoring Temple's comment, McNally addressed the boy very calmly. "Tell Etok that we don't want to wait here," he said. "Tell him that we want to follow him into battle."

The boy seemed to consider McNally's words for a long time. Then, finally turning with a shrug, he moved back out across the tundra to speak to the swaying wolf-man.

After another minute or two of nods and grunts, the shaman started out again, Temple and McNally following him at a distance of a few yards. When they finally drew in sight of the first shack, the wolf-man paused again to sniff the air. Then at last, cocking back his head, he let loose with his unearthly howl.

Old Pete sat very still, his eyes half-shut in dreamy concentration. On the ground in front of him lay a number of small, well-worn objects: the face of a wolf carved from walrus ivory, the petrified foot of an Arctic fox, the beak of a bird, a tiny bone-handled knife and a flashlight battery. The skin of a polar bear also lay in front of him.

"You have to be very quiet now," Irrigoo whispered. "It's very important to be quiet, or else he might lose his soul."

Able Team knelt in the gravel bed below the tiny rise where old Pete sat. Beside them sat Irrigoo, Elmer and four other men from the village. Although one of the whalers had told Maggie to wait in the shack with the rest of the women, when the cries of the wolf had begun to sound in the wind, she had also joined them.

"What do you mean, he might lose his soul?" Blancanales asked.

Irrigoo pressed a hand to his chest, then pointed to the sky. "To call down the spirit of the bear, he has to leave his body and go flying with the wind. If we make noise, he might get lost and then his own spirit won't be able to find the way back."

There were deep groans now sounding from the old Eskimo's chest, and his left hand seemed to move independently of his shoulder and arm, shaking spasmodically. Next, his right foot began to shiver, while his head jerked violently from side to side. Then, as another howl broke from deep within the fog, he suddenly rose to his haunches as if animated by some exterior force, as if yanked up by invisible strings.

"Now," Irrigoo whispered. "It's starting to happen now."

"What's starting to happen?" Schwarz whispered.

"The bear," Irrigoo replied. "The bear is upon him."

When the next cry of the wolf echoed out of the fog-drenched tundra, old Pete rose to his haunches, arching back until his body was bent like a bow and his jaws were taut with an undelivered roar....

And then he let it out.

It seemed to come from the ground below him, because his throat couldn't have possibly held that much sound: a deep and extended torrent of sound that literally hurt the ear drums.

"There, you see?" Irrigoo whispered. "You see?"

"See what?" Lyons whispered.

"He's become the bear. He's really become the bear."

"So what happens now?" Blancanales asked.

"Now we must not interfere," Irrigoo said.

Moments later, watching the old man lumber off with the bear skin over his shoulders, Lyons had to admit that there truly was something very different about him. Although he walked upright, his legs seemed heavier, slower. His head continued shifting from side to side, and there had been something very different about his eyes, about the way he worked his jaws.

"Are we just going to let him go out there alone?" Blancanales asked, watching as the man gradually vanished in the fog.

Lyons glanced at Maggie, but she merely shook her head. "Irrigoo is right," she said. "This is Eskimo business, and we can't interfere."

Blancanales shook his head and returned his gaze to the broad view of tundra and the fog. "This is crazy," he finally muttered.

But what he had just witnessed was not as crazy or as frightening as the maddened snarl of a wolf that suddenly alternated with the roar of a raging bear from deep within the wall of fog.

Lyons and his group halted among the thirty-foot columns of shore-fast ice, crouching low for cover as they heard the bear's roar and the snarling reply of the wolf once again. Although clearly frightened, Irrigoo and the five remaining Eskimo had refused to remain in the village when Lyons had decided to follow old Pete. Maggie had also refused to stay behind.

"Talk to me," Lyons demanded, turning to Maggie. "Tell me what the hell is going on out there."

The girl shook her head and continued to gaze out into the fog. "All I can tell you," she finally said, "is that these people have always had a very intense empathy with the earth and its animals. And sometimes, technically speaking, I guess you could say it leads to a kind of mental transformation."

"What the hell does that mean?" Blancanales asked.

"It means that as far as old Pete is concerned, he *is* that bear. He's not just acting it out, but he really *is* the bear."

"And the other one *is* a wolf?" Schwarz asked.

Maggie nodded. "Exactly."

"So what does it all mean?" Lyons questioned.

The woman shook her head again. "I'm not sure. According to some studies, it could lead to a whole new range of physical possibilities."

"Such as?"

"Radically increased strength and agility, heightened smell and vision, and sometimes even..."

"Even what?" Blancanales prodded.

"An inhuman ferocity and lust for blood."

"But they're not bulletproof, are they?" Schwarz asked.

"No."

"Then let's go get him," Blancanales suggested.

They moved out slowly and in a ragged line: Lyons and Blancanales slightly in the lead, followed by Schwarz, Maggie and the Eskimo. Although there were moments when the breeze seemed to cut the mist, for the most part they were surrounded by the fog.

Another series of snarling grunts broke from the mass of fog closer to the shore, and the Eskimo suddenly began speaking very quickly among themselves. Lyons held up a cautionary hand, but Irrigoo and his friends did not see it. They broke into a slow jog, still speaking among themselves and slipping their carbines off their shoulders.

"Tell them to hold back," Lyons whispered to Schwarz.

But having broken the rank, Irrigoo and the others had already begun climbing over the scattered blocks of ice along the shoreline.

"Hold them back!" Lyons shouted, suddenly conscious of another cry, a distinctly human cry of rage.

Another harsh voice broke from the fog-blanketed shore, and one of the Eskimo shouted, "There it is! Come on, there it is!"

But Lyons could see only the dim forms of the Eskimo climbing over the icy rubble.

Then, suddenly etched against the mist, one of the younger Eskimo began shuddering under the impact of the high-velocity fléchettes.

"It's a trick!" Irrigoo shouted, "Get back, it's a trick!"

But by now there were at least a dozen more fléchettes whistling out of the fog, and another Eskimo dropped to his knees, his mangled left arm whipping back and forth in the air. Then came a second and third salvo, and the wounded Eskimo collapsed into a bloody heap.

Maggie began screaming then, shaking her head in disbelief and staring at the still-shuddering vision of the dart-riddled whaler. Schwarz managed to drag her to the ice, but still couldn't keep her quiet, while someone close to him kept yelling, "I can't see! I can't see!"

And then, just as suddenly as the battle had begun, everything grew very still and silent for Carl Lyons. Even as the autofire continued cracking out of the fog and the Eskimo continued screaming in panicked fury, Lyons had isolated himself from that part of the firefight.

He rolled on his belly, hesitated three or four seconds, then finally ran forward. Beyond the field of ice-littered tundra lay a relatively open stretch of ground. From there a sloping plain of gravel led to the shore, where the first of Irrigoo's whalers had fallen.

Two Eskimo lay huddled behind the crumbling blocks of ice near the shoreline, their weapons lost, their hands pressed to their ears against the sound of whistling darts. Not far away, Irrigoo was yelling for his men to pull back.

Then, very calmly, very softly, Lyons heard Schwarz's voice behind him. "I think they're up that ridge, ol' buddy. You copy?"

Lyons turned and saw that the electronics wizard was belly-down among the icy rubble to his left. "Yeah," he replied. "I copy."

"So how do you want to play it?" Schwarz asked.

Lyons glanced to his right, saw that Blancanales had also managed to come up unseen through the fog, and suddenly he couldn't suppress a grin. "Straight," he said. "I want to play it straight."

Lyons kept two primary thoughts in his mind as he started moving out. To begin with, he told himself that despite everything else—despite the wolf-man and the bear-man, the magic songs and the chanting—winning this war still came down to easily comprehendible factors: velocity, trajectory, rate of fire and response to impact.

His second thought concerned the firing sequence of the Steyr and the hit probability of those 9.85-grain carbon steel darts. Although clearly advantageous in many respects, those advantages could also become a liability. With a faster firing sequence and a greater hit probability, the shooter was generally more inclined to expose himself for a longer period of time. And if he's exposed, Lyons told himself, he could be tagged with the deer rifle in one clean shot.

There were cries of the wolf again, but Lyons ignored it. This is between me and those Steyrs, he told himself. This is about trajectory, drift estimations and a 0.23-second time lapse between muzzle and target at three hundred yards.

He hesitated again as he approached the long shadow of the ice ridge. The ice is like the earth's crust, Maggie had told him. The movement was slow, but the pressures were enormous. It explained the massive ridge of blue-gray ice that rose twenty feet above the shore. It accounted for the deep groan beneath the surface of the sea, and the occasional cascade of crumbling blocks.

It was the little pressures that Lyons was most interested in now: the pressure of the actuator spring and the feeder arm that brings another fléchette into play.

Six more screaming fléchettes cut through the air above Lyons's head, but he was fairly certain that the salvos were blind and not directed at him. He was also fairly certain that the shooter was midway up the ridge, perched on a narrow ledge between two higher projections of ice. Yet it wasn't until the next fast salvo screamed out of the foggy shadows that he actually saw the man: squat and dark within the ice.

He scanned the terrain and calculated the distance for a full thirty seconds. Then, very slowly he started crawling forward. He moved with his weight on his knees and his elbows, the rifle resting in the crook of his elbows. Although a fair amount of moisture had finally seeped through his snow pants, he kept telling himself that the cold didn't matter. All that mattered was the wind drift, the fog and his own sense of timing.

He waited another eight or nine seconds before crawling into the deeper shadows. Then, again very slowly he crossed the last thirty feet to the icy litter directly below the ridge.

Several last-minute thoughts passed through Lyons's mind before he rose to fire. He thought about the steel darts and wondered if they lacked the individual accuracy that traditionally characterized fléchettes. He thought about the fact that fléchettes tend to hold their shape for deep penetration into hard targets, but tend to deform and tumble in soft targets. He also thought about the velocity and the searing pain.

But when he finally rose, sighting for that gray figure crouched along the icy crag, he really wasn't thinking about anything, except doing it... *doing it*.

He shot for what looked like the head, saw a dark spray of blood on the ice, but realized the shooter hadn't gone down. He squeezed off a second shot for the chest, but saw only a cloud of white ice. Then, although obviously crippled and in pain, the shooter began returning fire.

The first three fléchettes chewed the ice above Lyons's head, while the second salvo tore at the ice at his feet. But even as the muzzle flashed a third time, Lyons had already begun to squeeze the trigger again.

He shot for what he thought was the shooter's stomach, saw the flashing muzzle swing in a wild arc and heard a grunt of pain. He shot a fourth time for the ribs and saw the dark form tumble from the icy ledge. Then he heard nothing, except the foul wheezing of another sucking wound.

JACK TEMPLE LAY on his back, gazing up at the sky. He knew there was blood in his lungs, and that very soon he'd be dead. It was now just a question of going out in style.

He managed to rise to an elbow as Lyons approached, to rise and smile with a painful nod. He also managed to catch a glimpse of his Steyr, but knew that he didn't have the strength to pick it up again.

"How the hell are you?" he whispered.

Lyons took a long moment to study Temple's face. "Long time no see, Jack."

"Yeah." Temple smiled. "Long time."

"Where's your buddy?"

"You mean McNally?"

Lyons nodded again, watching the man's eyes very carefully as he shifted his gaze to the ridge above. Lyons nodded again as Temple glanced out to the shadows between two icy blocks. But it wasn't until Temple's lips spread into another thin smile that Lyons actually started moving again.

He rolled for the darker patch of ground, because that's where Temple's Steyr lay. He rolled shoulder first, discarding the deer rifle and taking the impact with his arm. Then, picking up the Steyr and praying that the magazine wasn't empty, he turned the roll into an awkward spin and came up firing.

Lyons fired from the hip as McNally emerged from the shadows. He fired two fast salvos into the shadows sixty feet beyond the ridge, then squeezed off a third salvo when he finally saw McNally's face. He heard McNally scream his name and saw McNally's Steyr flash. But at the same time he also saw McNally's chest explode with blood as at least three flechettes cut through the man's parka and pulverized his torso.

Lyons rose to his feet again very slowly. Although he couldn't see Temple's face, he knew the man was dead. Just as he knew that McNally was still alive... struggling to fill his blood-choked lungs with air.

McNally looked much worse than Lyons had imagined, the blood spreading out across the ice, his left leg chewed to a pulp.

"Pretty shitty place to die, ain't it?" McNally wheezed as Lyons stepped into view.

The Able Team warrior glanced around him at the fog-shrouded landscape, at the ghostly ridge of ice in the sky.

"I can think of worse," he replied. "I can think of a lot of worse places."

Lyons moved another three or four steps closer to the man, then knelt by McNally's side to examine the wound. After only a glance, however, he knew that McNally didn't stand a chance: death was inevitable.

"What about Jackie-boy?" McNally asked after a momentary spasm of pain had passed. "Is Jackie-boy all right?"

Lyons shook his head. "No."

McNally shivered with another stab of pain, then shrugged. "Too bad. The kid had promise."

"Look, if you want me to try and get you..."

McNally merely smiled. "Hey, forget it. I wouldn't do the same for you. Besides, you'd better save your sympathy for yourself, because this one ain't over till the wolf sings...."

Although McNally continued to smile, he was no longer breathing.

For a long time after McNally had died, Lyons remained kneeling beside his body. He knelt in the shadow of the icy crag as daylight faded and darkness approached. Although the faint voices of villagers still continued to penetrate the fog, he felt completely alone. Then, by degrees, like the slow approach of sea mist, he sensed the wolf again.

He withdrew a fresh magazine from McNally's parka and picked up the Steyr. Although the wind was marginally stronger, it did nothing to dissipate the fog. Nor was the moon much help, not with the shadows from the ice mounds.

He heard what might have been Schwarz or Blancanales climbing down from the ridge but knew that his friends would not have approached quite that way.

Then, catching a glimpse of movement between two massive columns of ice, he lifted the Steyr to his shoulder and dropped the safety....

But the creature didn't attack from the ice; it came from the blackness above.

He felt the weight of it first, at least a hundred and fifty pounds dragging him down to the ice. He smelled the fetid breath and the stench of its fur. Lyons rolled on his side, desperately trying to shake it off, but it was part of him now, a furious shadow clinging to his back for the kill.

A single thought tore through his brain—remember, it's still basically human. But at the same time, he felt the fangs, at least four inches, rip through his parka and search for his throat.

He felt those four-inch fangs rake across his skull again, and warm blood dripped onto his face. He rolled on his left hip, wildly bucking and thrashing to throw the thing off, but the creature's strength was too much for him. Then, as he felt the cold intrusion of the fangs again, he finally realized that what old Pete had said was true. *Only magic could stop it.*

He began to lose consciousness; his vision was growing dim and his sense of time was beginning to fade. And then the bear appeared, and just as quickly as the wolf had been on him, it left him alone to face this new—and more formidable—threat.

For a long time, at least six or seven seconds, the two man-animals simply looked at one another: rampant and swaying, with slack jaws and dull stares. Finally tossing back its head with a shuddering roar, the bear lunged. He attacked with a quick feint, then moved to the left, swinging its great right claw. The wolf reared, twisting in midair, striking back with a flash of fangs. But having finally drawn a little blood, the bear was on him immediately.

The two creatures became one, separated, then merged again in a blurred ball of white. There were streaks of blood along the wolf's shoulder, more blood along the bear's jaw. At times the movements were distinctly human, yet there was nothing human in the voices, nothing even remotely human about the fury.

Lyons rolled on his side and reached for the Steyr. Not that the weapon had any real place in the conflict, not that he even knew what he was doing. But when the creatures briefly separated in a moment of panting rage, the Able Team warrior couldn't stop himself from injecting a little of the twentieth century into their primeval battle.

Lyons screamed as he fired, a scream that was no less enraged than the screams of those animal-men. But at the same time, the bear also renewed his screaming attack, lunging in with a swinging claw moments after the burst of fléchettes.

It was impossible to tell what finally brought down the wolf.

For a long time after the wolf had fallen, Lyons simply remained on his knees and looked at the thing. The bear had retreated to an icy rise above the shore, slowly taking on a somewhat more human shape as it whispered another tuneless song. There were also human voices growing stronger as they moved toward him from the ridge. Finally, laying down the Steyr and rising to his feet, Lyons limped over to the lifeless form and nudged it with the toe of his boot. He simply looked at it, examining the cleverly stitched folds of skin where the bullet-resistant vest had been concealed, examining the cleverly constructed face mask and the hand-held weapon designed to simulate the ripping fangs.

"Surprised?"

He turned to meet Maggie's weary gaze.

"No," he breathed. "I'm not surprised."

She took a step closer, then knelt down and picked up the weapon—stainless steel and serrated. "Not really part of the tradition," she said, "but effective."

He shrugged again, ripping the mask away to reveal a face still contorted with base rage. "Any idea who he was?" he asked.

"I think they used to call him Etok, Etok of the Seven Songs. Supposedly he was once one of the most powerful shamans, until it got away from him."

"So he brought it back with stainless-steel fangs and a bullet-proof vest, is that it?"

She nodded, still staring at the shaman's face, at the sightless eyes and the clenched teeth. "Yes, he brought it back with oil money."

Schwarz and Blancanales appeared, moving slowly out of the fog ahead of Irrigoo and the surviving Eskimo. When they neared the body, they stopped and hunkered down to the ice. Then, for a long time they, too, simply looked at the thing... while old Pete continued softly chanting on the rise above.

"Well, so much for the magic," Blancanales finally breathed. "Know what I mean?"

But after briefly meeting Maggie's gaze again and then glancing up to old Pete on the ridge, Lyons simply shook his head and smiled. "I wouldn't be too sure about that, Pol."

IT WAS NEARLY DAWN when Lyons and the others returned to the village. Although the fog still hung above the shore, the skies to the west had finally begun to clear. It was also beginning to clear along the southern stretch of tundra where the breeze smelled faintly of pines.

They sat on the floor of Irrigoo's home: Lyons, Schwarz, Blancanales and Maggie. Although there was food—canned sardines, pineapple and Spam and boiled walrus intestines—only Irrigoo, old Pete and other Eskimo were eating. The women remained in the kitchen whispering among themselves. Every now and again hysterical cries of grief broke from one of the neighboring shacks where the widows of those who had died sat in mourning.

"How can we ever thank you," Maggie began, breaking the silence that filled the room as each person reflected on the battle.

Lyons took a long pull from a bottle of Jack Daniel's, then ran his sleeve across his mouth. "No," he finally replied. "Don't thank us. It's not over, not by a long shot."

Maggie reached for the bottle, then also took a hard pull. "Oh, I think we all know that."

"Not that we're suggesting that you give up," Schwarz added. "If you throw in the towel now, these people are finished."

"Oh, I don't intend to throw in the towel," Maggie sighed. "Hell, I intend to fight those greedy oilmen in every court in the land, and then keep on fighting through appeals, if necessary. I also intend to ram the ice-floe variables right down their throats, and scream about the *ivu* factor all the way to Washington. But nothing I do is going to keep these people alive, not in the long run. Because if oil means anything up here, it means that the old ways are over, that these people are doomed and that their land will probably die with them. It also means that the consortium will just keep getting richer, and that guys like Sweeny and Denton will just keep laughing their heads off at how they scared the dumb Eskimo with a guy in a wolf suit. And if that sounds cynical, I'm sorry. But it happens to be the truth."

"Except for the part about Sweeny and Denton," Lyons said. "Something tells me that that part isn't true."

Maggie put down the whiskey bottle and looked at him. "What are you talking about?" she asked suspiciously.

But Lyons did not reply. Instead, he simply shifted his gaze to the end of the room where old Pete had suddenly begun to sing again—gently rocking back and forth while softly singing another tuneless song.

37

Sweeny jammed a fresh magazine into his CAR-15 and told the driver to stop the limo. Although the gold-plated, fully automatic weapon was hardly designed for hunting game animals, he simply couldn't resist the temptation, not with the caribou just standing there looking at him.

"This is crazy," Denton said. "We're supposed to be getting the hell out of the country. We're not supposed to be bagging trophies."

Sweeny merely smiled. "I don't want the trophy, ol' buddy. I just want to kill it."

It was dusk, another gray-blue dusk with yet another ice fog rolling in from the bay. Yet the moment the limo had rounded the turn, the caribou had still been clearly visible in the headlights, big-shouldered and defiant.

"Anyway," Sweeny muttered as he climbed out of the limousine, "this is only going to take a minute."

He moved out slowly, breathing deeply and savoring the moment. Although shooting caribou from the roadside was not nearly as satisfying as shooting wolves from a chopper, a kill was still a kill, and it always made him feel good.

The animal simply watched for the first fifty yards of Sweeny's approach, standing stock-still on a hillock of moss. Then, apparently sensing the hunter's intention, it lumbered onto the darker ground between the mounds of Arctic grass.

The continual echo and throb of machinery along this stretch of tundra had made the wildlife increasingly timid. But Sweeny had the distinct impression that this animal was not afraid at all, that it was purposely leading him into the darker ground, and that was a challenge he could not ignore.

He caught another fleeting glimpse of the animal as it loped into the long shadows cast by the storage tanks. For a moment he saw and heard nothing, nothing except the wind through thin stalks of grass and the faint clang of machinery from the oil compounds. Somewhat closer to the darker ground, he also heard what may have been the soft tread of a second animal. But he did not think anything of it until he saw the ragged silhouette.

At first glance he assumed the second animal was a dog, probably one of the oil-field dogs that had managed to escape the compound. But something about the shape of its head and the slope of its jaw told him that it wasn't a dog.

He hesitated, inching his hand along the breech of his weapon and dropping the safety. He suddenly realized that the beast was too large to be a dog...much too large.

Sweeny felt the trace of a chill along his spine and a sudden emptiness in his stomach. He was also suddenly cold, literally shivering in the breeze as the creature drew closer...

Yet it wasn't until Lyons rose up on his haunches, slack jawed and hollow eyed, that Sweeny began to scream.